THE PREMORTALS

JACQUELINE WRENLEY

Copyright © 2020 JACQUELINE WRENLEY YAP

All rights reserved

The characters and events portrayed in this book are fictitious. Any similarity to real persons, living or dead, is coincidental and not intended by the author.

No part of this book may be reproduced, or stored in a retrieval system, or transmitted in any form or by any means, electronic, mechanical, photocopying, recording, or otherwise, without express written permission of the publisher.

Ebook by Jacqueline Wrenley Yap
Tagbilaran City, Bohol
Philippines

wrenley007@gmail.com

CONTENTS

Title Page	1
Copyright	2
CHAPTER 1: Fortis	7
CHAPTER 2: Coastal City	33
CHAPTER 3: Homecoming	53
CHAPTER 4: The Pledge	80
CHAPTER 5: Lost Souls	115
CHAPTER 6: First Village	129
CHAPTER 7: Revelations	147
CHAPTER 8: Wild Horses	161
CHAPTER 9: The Game	170
CHAPTER 10: Blackard	177
CHAPTER 11: Impulse	194
CHAPTER 12: Consequences	199
CHAPTER 13: Homeward	206
CHAPTER 14: Gelhem	216
About The Author	233

"OUR LAWS MADE LOVE A GAMBLE, YOU WERE ONE OF THE FORTUNATE IF YOU FOUND LOVE AFTER MARRIAGE."

CHAPTER 1: FORTIS

CURTIS

Staying in this room was my routine for the last twelve years but this would be my last day of learning and training befitting my station and then we would finally be released back to society. Before all that though, I have to be here one more time early in the morning while Professor Hughes starts the day by discussing the subject we already knew.

"Well my Lords, I'm sure you are all excited to go back home tomorrow."

"More excited of our grand party tonight!" Lord Stephen interrupted with a chuckle while the class cheered on.

"Alright, quiet down my Lords, in the meantime, you are all stuck here with me," Professor Hughes replied with a grin," Let's begin."

A few of us started to get uncomfortable on our chairs, bracing for another boring lecture.

"I'll make this quick since all of you are already familiar with the subject matter. I am here to refresh your memory since this is required by the law before you all rejoin society. Do not hesitate to ask questions along the way," stated Professor Hughes in his serious tone. "First, the stations," Professor Hughes continued, "There are seven, what are they?"

Everybody knew the answer to this question but no one was willing to raise their hand to answer.

"Lord Stephen?" Professor Hughes looked at the direction where Stephen was seated. He gave a look of what seems to be boredom but answered the question anyway,

"The Sovereigns, The Elites, Alphas, Betas, The Corps, Deltas and The Omegas," then straightened his black blazer uniform proud of himself.

"Good, it seems that you've been paying attention to your classes after all," the Professor remarked which made the class laugh.

"The Sovereigns are our Emperor, the Empress, and the crowned Prince. The Elites are the Dukes and Duchesses, Prince and Princesses, the Ladies and Lords which are all of you until some of you will become Dukes one day." The class gave another cheer. "The Alphas," the Professor continued, "are the very wealthy businessmen and successful professionals, or owners of large firms and enterprises, political leaders, and high ranking military officers. The Betas are the average earning professionals, in skills or in talents and small business owners, while the Deltas… who would like to continue?" the Professor scanned the room to see who would be willing to volunteer, "Lord Timothy?"

Timothy was reluctant to answer but he cleared his throat and spoke," The Deltas are the servants of the Sovereigns and the Elites; and the Omegas are for the labor and services. The Corps are the military and the Protectors."

The Professor nodded in approval, "Well done my Lord, now on to the tricky part," he was pacing in front of the class, "Marriage, what age are we all eligible?"

Someone shouted twenty at the back of the room.

"Good," the Professor complimented to no one in particular.

"But that age does not apply to us right Professor?" Stephen asked, "Sovereigns, Elites and sometimes the Alphas may wish to marry as early as eighteen or in other words, as soon as we get out of here," Stephen declared with a sneer.

"True," the Professor responded, "As soon as you turn eighteen and you have graduated from this institute, you may be eligible for marriage after you rejoin society. The law has a few exceptions to the higher stations who can afford to create a family. But for the Betas, the Corps, Deltas, and Omegas, they have to wait until they are twenty to be eligible to marry for reasons that they are given two years after they graduate to search for an occupation. All citizens of the Empire regardless of station are eligible to marry; it's just a matter of time and compatibility."

"Now, who chooses who will marry who?" the Professor was looking at my direction, I held my breath for my name to be called, "Lord Curtis?"

"The Numen System," I answered as quickly as I could to get it over with.

"That's right. This computer system was created to choose the most compatible mates physically and genetically that are not blood related to create order and to put an end to genetically passed diseases and abnormalities. The mates are chosen at random depending on their station of course. Every station is subject to the Numen System except for the Sovereigns who have the freewill to choose."

"Yeah right!" Stephen interjected but the Professor just briefly looked at him and ignored his reaction.

It was not part of the topic or open for discussion but most of us knew that the Elites and sometimes the very wealthy Alphas use their connections and wealth to bribe a Numen Chief Programmer to manually override a match and they can choose who their sons or daughters can marry. They make deals to other families to match their children to gain more wealth and expand their enterprises for the Alphas; and to have more lands, prestige, and alliances for the Elites. This kind of practice was against the law but most of the Elites and some of the Alphas were peers to the Emperor, if they get caught, the Protectors just turned a blind eye. The Chief Programmer was more than willing to break a few laws for them just to receive a very large amount of money.

Professor Hughes went over to his desk and sat down on the chair and looked over a couple of his notes before proceeding, "We're done with how mates are chosen, now, let's continue with the marriage station limitations."

Some of us were starting to fall asleep with the morning lecture, all of this was taught to us on our first year in the institute and the proceeding years as if they feared we might forget.

"The Sovereigns can marry whoever they want regardless of station," he continued.

It was funny if you think about it, the Emperor or the Crowned Prince have the power to marry whoever they want regardless of station but they only chose from the Sovereigns of other Empires or from the Elites, and on rare occasions the Alphas. They might as well place some limitations on their station as well.

"The Elites," continued the Professor, "are matched with the Elites and the Alphas."

"Is it true Professor that there came a time when an Elite was matched with a Beta?" the interruption made us looked at the Lord with a blond hair and gray eyes seated next to me.

"Yes Lord Ambrose I believed so, it had only happened

twice in recorded history. The Chief Programmer once explained that the Numen System will generate a match for an Elite with the Beta station when no other match is possibly found on the Elite and Alpha pool since there are only a few of them. The system will automatically choose a Beta with identical or almost the same genetic characteristics of an Alpha or Elite."

"That will never happen to first born Elites, heir to a Duke," Stephen sneered.

Ambrose glared at him with disgust for his lack of sensitivity. His tactless behavior made him forget that Professor Hughes is a Beta, or maybe he just didn't care.

"Do not worry my Lords. This almost never happens," the professor reassured us while continuing to ignore Stephen's side remark.

I was contemplating on Professor Hughes' words, this never happens but it did. Only the Elites were rich and powerful enough to reverse the match if it did happen by paying the Chief Programmer to change the result especially when the match was a Duke or heir to a Duke. But when it did happen, the Elites considered it as a joke, a laughing spectacle from what I had heard. They say that this was the most expensive bribe an Elite had to pay.

"Let us move on, the Alphas are matched with the Elites and other Alphas."

"The Betas as matched with other Betas and the Corps," the Professor went on, "The Corps who are drafted according to their physical attributes and strength are matched with the Betas. The Deltas are matched with other Deltas and Omegas. Lastly, the Omegas are matched with Deltas and other Omegas. These matches with the stations were designed to improve and preserve the skills and talents for the future generations to come and to create order."

"Professor?" Nigel who was sitting in front of the class was raising his hand.

"Yes Lord Nigel?"

Nigel pushed the rim of his glasses to his nose before answering, "What about promotion to a higher station? Could we run it again?"

"There are three ways to be promoted; it is by the Emperor's choice, or being drafted for the Corps, or by marriage. An example would be in the military Corps, when a soldier exhibits qualities deserving of a high ranking officer or a political leader, the Emperor may promote him making him an Alpha, this is the only way for someone in the Corps to be promoted. Or when an Omega enlists or was drafted for the Corps and passed the test then they would be promoted to the Corps. The promotion through marriage is understandable by itself. The Deltas are of higher rank than the Omegas. If an Omega is matched by a Delta, he or she would be promoted and leave his or her previous occupation and would render their life in servitude to the Emperor and his royal household, or the Elites. The child from a Beta and Corps parents would be tested first whether he or she would belong to the Beta or the Corps. Is this clear to you Lord Nigel?" the Professor explained glancing at Nigel with a smile.

"Yes Professor," was his shy reply.

"What happens Professor if the Numen System does not have a match for someone?" it was Timothy's turned to ask.

Professor Hughes took his time to answer, "There are instances that the Numen System will take a long time to find a match, or will never find one at all."

"You mean some may never marry?" Timothy inquired further.

"Yes Lord Timothy, the Numen System is a very complicated program that we will never understand why for some they will never find a match, and when you are over fifty, you lose that eligibility."

"Could it be just a glitch or a mistake?" Leonas interrupted who was seated at the back row.

"I highly doubt it Lord Leonas, the System is flawless and has been even before you and I were born. Some may never find a match because as you remember, the main purpose of the Numen System is to make matches with men and women who are genetically compatible. Maybe some do not have someone they are compatible with out there. We are all eligible but it does not mean all will find a match." Professor Hughes explained.

The topic was getting interesting that some of the Lords were obviously having more questions in their minds as well.

"So what can they do?" Ambrose asked.

"Nothing Lord Ambrose, they continue to live their lives alone. It is against the law to have any form of intimate relations with anyone without being married first. If caught, they will be sentenced to ten years in prison if they are unmarried, but adultery is punishable by death just like murderers and traitors."

The Professor paused then finally said, "Anymore questions before I proceed?" he was searching the room for more raised hands but there was only silence.

"Okay, if there are no more questions, let us proceed then to our last topic of the day which is the child allocation," the Professor started pacing again.

"Each station is allocated with a certain number for

children they are allowed to have. This law has been approved since the beginning of our Empire to solve the overpopulation problem back then. All of us men and women, with no exceptions, are to be born sterile and thanks to the medical breakthrough of our forefathers, we are born not from our mothers but from a Womb Simulated Environment Chamber or the WSEC or simply called the Birth Chamber. We are not conceived by the union of two reproductive cells like the barbaric age but with the fusion of two compatible blood and a few basic genetic modifications to prevent birth defects and ensure healthy offspring. This is where the child allocation law comes into place, each station is allowed how many children? Anyone? Yes Lord Marcus?"

"The Sovereigns are allowed four children, the Elites three, and the Alphas can have two, while the rest are only allowed one child," responded Marcus seemingly sure of himself.

"Correct Lord Marcus, there are more Beta, Deltas, Corps and Omegas that is why they are allowed only one child."

"My father once told me that the Sterility Serum was also needed for the infant to grow in a Birth Chamber," Stephen blurted out.

We were all looking at Professor Hughes waiting for a respond, "Yes Lord Stephen, without the Serum an embryo will not survive the early stage of development," the Professor calmly replied.

The Professor looked at Stephen then said, "Your father is a great man, he knows more than I do".

Stephen's face was beaming with pride.

"Well then," Professor Hughes was leaning on his desk changing the topic, "What age are the children sent to the

Institutions?"

He was looking at the raised hand at the back corner of the room.

"Yes Lord Chaste?"

"Six years old."

"Indeed Lord Chaste, at six years old, all female children are sent to the Yuvaika Institute to learn and train according to their station while all six year old male children are sent here at Fortis Institute where all of you would spend the next twelve years of your life. All parents regardless of station, must comply to this law and send their children to these institutes until they graduate at eighteen and be ready to go back to society," the Professor paused and crossed his arms, "Now who could recall where the names of the Institutes came from?" he continued.

Hands were raised simultaneously this time, probably because it was an easy question. The professor chose the Lord seated behind me this time.

"Yes?"

"Yuvaika was named after our very first Empress and Fortis from our first Emperor."

"You're absolutely right my Lord," the Professor nodded in agreement.

"Emperor Fortis and Empress Yuvaika were our very first Sovereigns," he resumed, "The Institutes were created after the Great War to promote peace and to make sure that the war will never happen again." He paused for a moment then began pacing the room, "Now who could tell me what the Great War was about? Lord Curtis?"

I hesitated for a bit then answered the best I could, "The Great War was about men versus the women."

Professor Hughes smiled, "Continue my Lord."

I shifted on my seat, "It was about who was the better gender, and disputes on equality and rights, and among others. The war lasted for more than a century. Emperor Fortis was the leader of the men faction while Empress Yuvaika was for the women. When the two finally settled for peace, they formed an alliance through marriage to erase any hostility from their loyal subjects, and to seal the bond, they had children who continued to become Sovereigns and Elites. They created the laws and the stations with the help of their appointed councils made up mostly of their loyal followers who later became Elites and given the titles Dukes and Duchesses, and were given lands to establish their Dukedom. The new laws and way of life was set up to create order among the citizens. The Institutes were built to separate the boys and the girls at a crucial age to prevent any discrimination and to discourage any thoughts of gender dominance or partial treatment or misplaced affections making sure not to make the same mistakes we once did before," I let out a sigh of relief hoping that I answered it right.

Professor Hughes gave a huge grin which made me feel contented of my answer.

"I couldn't have said it better, you'd make an excellent Lord," he declared directly at me. He went over to his desk again and shuffle some papers, "It seems that we are at the end of our discussion my Lords," while still looking down at his papers.

The class started to move in their seats with enthusiasm.

"Before we go, any last questions?"

There were none.

"None? Then congratulations my Lords, we have reached the end of our time together. I hope none of you grew tired of me."

The class laughed with the Professor. "After twelve years, which I am sure is a lifetime for some of you, make you feel unsure of what you are going to do outside these walls but fear not, once you leave this place tomorrow, your new life as Lords awaits you and I am sure you will all be successful in whatever you do," Professor Hughes spoke with confidence and reassurance. He paused briefly and took one final look at us, "I hereby proclaim this as the end of our session, you are all dismissed."

Everyone clapped their hands and cheered as we all stood up and started to leave the room. It was starting to empty as I was about to leave, and on my way pass Professor Hughes' desk, he called my name and said, "You were quiet in class today Lord Curtis, is everything alright?"

I stopped in front of him, I did not know how to answer, and there had been a lot on my mind lately especially regarding tomorrow. I was finally going home but I wasn't looking forward to it and I had no idea what to expect after being away for so long. I fear that home might be a new place for me but I wasn't going to tell him that.

"Everything is fine Professor, I'm just excited to be going home that's all," I lied hoping that I sounded convincing enough.

Professor Hughes smiled at me, "I know the feeling. The great opportunities that awaits the young," he sighed, "Congratulations on being top of your class Lord Curtis. Your speech at the graduation ceremony was truly inspiring. I'm glad there are still Lords like you," he continued.

"Thank you Professor, I learned from great teachers," I told him with a tone full of gratitude.

He smiled and said, "Well, I won't keep you. Good bye Lord Curtis and good luck."

I slightly nodded my head and smiled back at him as a way of saying good bye before I left the room. I must admit, I would miss the Professor, he was the closest thing to a father to us while we stayed at the Institute. I learned a lot from him as our class director. Ambrose was waiting for me by the hallway. I went to him and as I came closer he asked, "What was that all about?"

"Nothing, just saying our goodbyes," I replied.

"Well, I have to say, I'm going to miss the Professor when we leave," Ambrose confessed and I grinned at his remark.

"Let's go have some lunch at the dining hall shall we?" I suggested.

"Okay," Ambrose replied.

We were walking down the hallway while Ambrose was talking about going home. We've been good friends since we first arrived and we had been inseparable ever since. He told me once that he thinks of me as his brother and the feeling was mutual. I do not blame him though, since he had only two older sisters. His father, Lord Brider Craye, Duke of Blackard, one of the richest Dukedom in the Empire that was rich in oil, decided to have two daughters because he was simply fond of daughters than sons in where an Elite society would prefer sons over daughters. Then he had Ambrose his only son to inherent all his lands someday. Ambrose's sisters were all married, so I could imagine the anticipation of Lord Craye upon the return of his only heir. I think Ambrose would make a great Duke someday, a fair and just Lord. We were on our way to the dining hall when Stephen decided to join us uninvited.

"Well, if it isn't the heir and the spare," proclaimed Stephen in his arrogant voice. Ambrose gave Stephen the dirty look. He never liked Stephen for always referring me as the spare, brother to the Duke of Pinewood. Stephen's opinion was that if you're not the heir, then you're useless. Easy for him to say, Stephen was the heir to the Duke of Sunglow, whose lands were rich in gold, making them the wealthiest family in the Elite station. Stephen was completely the opposite of Ambrose though. He had long light brown hair and light brown eyes, he was loud and obnoxious yet no one would dare displease him. His influential father, Lord Syrus Rectner was one of the Emperor's closest peers making Stephen immune to almost anything unfavorable and he knew it.

"So what are you two losers doing after you get out of here?" Stephen sneered as he came between us and placed his arms around our shoulders. I pushed his arm feeling disgusted and replied, "It's none of your business Stephen," then I straightened my white collar under the blazer.

Ambrose slapped Stephen's arm away and added, "As if you cared anyway."

He ignored our actions and respond and spoke coolly to us, "My father is already making plans for a match for me, a woman from a very wealthy Elite and he made sure that she is gorgeous," he had a grin on his face, "Once the arrangement are all done, we will be married and I cannot wait to seal the bond if you guys know what I mean," he added with a wink.

"You're disgusting!" Ambrose snapped.

Stephen shrugged his shoulders, "What else is there?" he continued, "I pity the fool who would marry out of random from the Numen System." He lowered his voice

as if he was going to tell us a secret, "I heard some would have matches with someone they could not even bear to look at and some would sleep in separate rooms throughout their entire marriage. Not even bothering to be intimate to each other, even loathing their mates. Tsk! Such a pity."
He was assuming that it would happen to us.
"Well boys good luck on your marriages. I am sure it would be a happy one," he said with a sarcastic tone, "Don't worry Curtis, your marriage would not matter to your Dukedom anyway," he ended with a loud sarcastic laugh and left us without giving us a chance to react. Ambrose face was nothing but anger staring at Stephen as he left, "Don't listen to him Curtis. You know very well your marriage would matter to your brother to form alliances with other Elites and Alphas," he said with encouragement.

"I am not worried Ambrose, marriage is far from my mind right now," I assured him and I hope I do not marry soon, I don't think I would be ready.

"And besides, Andrew would make sure I would have a suitable match," I lied to him. The truth was, my brother and I were never really close, not like what I had with Ambrose. I did not know what my brother had in store for me but I doubt it would be for my best interest. Since he became Duke of Pinewood, our home, it was all about him. Being the Duke and head of our family, the House of Bermule, after father passed away, he had control over my well-being and everything else. And being brother to a Duke, I was obliged to follow and be loyal to him. I felt bad lying to Ambrose but I didn't need him to worry about me.

"Yeah," Ambrose acknowledged, "But wouldn't it be

great though to marry for love?" he admitted.

I nodded in agreement, "it would be a great thing," I paused, searching for the proper words to say to him. "I'm sure you'd marry and the two of you would fall in love Ambrose, you're a great man, women would fall easily for you," I exclaimed with a chuckle to ease the seriousness of the conversation. I meant what I said to him and I hoped he would find a match that would make him happy because he deserved it but I couldn't help the feeling of uncertainty since love was a luxury that was not easy or may be impossible to have. Our laws made love a gamble, you were one of the fortunate if you found love after marriage.

We arrived at the dining hall, all the other Elites were already having their lunch. I saw Nigel standing up and waving at us, gesturing us that he saved us a seat with him. I waved and smiled back in respond. We approached Nigel and sat at the empty seats beside him on the long table.

"Hey Nigel," I greeted him with a smile.

"Hey guys, what took you so long?" he asked pushing the rim of his glasses to his nose.

"We encountered an unwelcomed pest along the hallway," explained Ambrose with a grin.

Nigel looked puzzled with his statement.

"Never mind, what are we having today?" Ambrose changed the subject.

Once we took our seats, the footmen with their long red coats served us with our soup as the first part of the meal. There were other dining halls in the Fortis Institute but the Elite's was the finest, second to the Sovereign's. Each station had their own separate wing inside the walls of the Institution, each containing its own classrooms, gym, dining hall, dormitories, training areas, and others. The Omegas, Deltas, and Betas had a larger wing since they have more population than us. They also had more facilities because they had a vaster field of choices in their occupation. The Alphas were trained in their chosen profession, or how to run a business, or in politics. The Elites were taught about business also and on how to run a Dukedom. The Sovereigns were rarely present since it consists of only one family and all were pass the age of eighteen. The Crowned Prince and his siblings were usually sent to their very own private wing where they were educated under a private Alpha tutors taught on how to rule an Empire and other important royal responsibilities. Most of our teachers here were Betas like Professor Hughes and they were trained in the professional field of education. Meanwhile, the Corps which includes the Protectors, had their own separate training ground focusing on military and law enforcement, and they had one of the largest wing. None of the stations were allowed to mingle with someone from another station but it was not unusual though that some Omegas would befriend a Beta, or an Alpha would be friendly to an Elite. As for me, I do not know anyone here at Fortis who was outside my station except for the faculty of course. The Yuvaika Institute was of a different area but not far from here. It had similar facilities and lay out as the Fortis, and no men were allowed to enter, it goes the same way here too for the women. We exited the dining hall after we finished our lunch. Nigel was with us this time. We became friends with Nigel during our later years in the institution. He belonged to a minor House whose family were smart just like him. He was second best in class after me but I think he would have been first if the pressure didn't took hold of him. We remained friends though, that's what makes Nigel a true one of a kind companion. He had brown short hair that shines in the light and his blue eyes like mine were hidden behind his spectacles. He was also short, that's why Stephen was fond of bullying him so we took him under our protection.

"So are you guys going to the party tonight?" Nigel asked the both of us.

"Definitely I'm going," Ambrose said sounding excited.

"I'm not sure exactly," Nigel hesitated.

"Huh? Why not? It will be fun," Ambrose encouraged.

"Come on Nigel, it's our last day, we may never spend a night like this together," I said trying to persuade him.

"I don't know," Nigel paused, "You know how I hate social parties," he explained.

"Don't worry, Curtis and I will never leave your side the whole time," Ambrose trying to reassure Nigel. "And besides," I added, "We need to get you drunk before we send you home," I winked at Nigel. They both laughed and we knew Nigel was convinced he was going to have a time of his life tonight.

I was standing on the hallway near the huge entrance doors waiting for the man servant to bring my things down from my room. I woke up that morning with a terrible hangover from all the drinks and late partying last night. I could barely stand with this headache and the people around going about their business in the hall getting ready to leave and saying their goodbyes was only making the pain worst. It was passed midday, everybody in the Elite station who attended the party woke up late. I went out the main doors to get some fresh air which did some good. I was standing with my back towards the door when I felt a gentle pat on my back.

"Are you okay?"

I turned around, it was Ambrose, fresh as ever as if he had a good night sleep and all those alcohol last night didn't bother him one bit.

"I'm fine, feeling a bit dizzy that's all," I responded.

Ambrose smiled then happily added, "It's all worth it though, we had a blast last night."

Just as he said it, Nigel appeared who looked worse than me. He came to where we were standing using all that he had to keep himself from falling.

"Hey guys," Nigel greeted weakly.

Ambrose laughed, "Here is the man of the night. If only you could see yourself last night Nigel, you wouldn't believe that it was you," he patted Nigel on the back.

"Last night would be the last time I would ever drink that much," Nigel declared trying to speak with dignity.

"Not unless we meet again Nigel," Ambrose teased.

A car pulled over the driveway and the driver went out his side and opened the door of the back passenger seat.

"That's my ride," Nigel stated as we fell silent.

Ambrose was the first one to speak, "Good luck Nigel," he stretched out his hand to him.

Nigel shook it while saying, "Thanks Ambrose, I do hope we'll see each other again."

Nigel then released his hand and turned to face me. I offered my hand to him and sadly said, "Don't be a stranger, you hear?" Nigel took it and we shook hands.

"Never. Thank you for everything Curtis. You've been a great help."

We exchanged smiles and Nigel started going down the stairs from the main door to the car, giving us one last look before he went in the car and waved good bye. We waved back as his driver closed the door and returned to his seat, and drove off.

Another car stopped by the driveway, and the driver opened the passenger door at the back. A familiar face stepped out from the car, a woman in her early fifties with black hair and some traces of white tied neatly in a bun gave me the warmest smile, it was Miss Pattilyn.

I looked at Ambrose which I am certain he saw the sign of sadness on my face as the inevitable was happening. "This is me," I declared.

Ambrose never took his eyes away from me and nodded in silence. He offered his hand to shake and said, "No matter where you are, know this that I am always here to help you if ever you needed it my friend."

It took me a while to respond, but I finally shook his hand firmly and solemnly said, "You're more like a brother to me than my brother I have back home. I wouldn't know what to do without your encouragement constantly reminding me."

Ambrose let out a low laugh and gave me a brief hug and let go to face me one more time, "You're ready Curtis, more than you know. You know where to find me."

I smiled and jokingly said, "Oh I hope I won't find you in a bar somewhere."

He laughed as I made my way down the car while the driver took my luggage and stored them in the trunk. Miss Pattilyn went inside the car first. I gave Ambrose one last look and waved goodbye and he did the same. The driver closed the door after I went in and we drove off.

We left the institute and it was a good day to come home, with the sun shining and everything was peaceful as I was staring out the window. I was thankful that

Miss Pattilyn gave me time to myself and my thoughts. She was always a thoughtful woman. For twelve years, we were never allowed outside the walls of the Institute except for emergencies or an event that requires our presence. Fortis was located outside a nearby city surrounded by mountains and trees. Nothing had changed much outside the walls since I first came here. The laws of the Empire helped protect these natural resources, having almost depleted once by overpopulation and the Great War and because of these laws in placed that they were in abundance once more, and thick forest runs all over the country side outside the cities, everywhere an ocean of greens.

"We'll be arriving at the shuttle dock in an hour my Lord," informed Miss Pattilyn breaking the silence.

I didn't respond, still preoccupied with my thoughts. Miss Pattilyn had been with my family since before my brother and I were even born. Being a Delta, she became our nanny and had been like a mother when my own mother passed away when I was only six before I was sent for Fortis, and Andrew was sixteen. She had been my comfort when father shut himself away when mother was gone and he had never been the same ever since. I was never close to my father, he never showed any affection and only spoke to me when needed. He would rather prefer the company of my brother, Andrew. My father never visited me while I was in Fortis, not like the other parents who went to see their sons on a regular basis. Only Miss Pattilyn had visited me weekly without fail, always bringing me something sweet to eat from back home and good news, or how the household were missing me, their little Lord. She would always smile during her visits, always willing to hear what I had been doing in the

Institution. She would defend my father when I asked why he didn't come to visit. She would say that father was busy running the Dukedom with my brother and that he would try to visit me the next time, which never happened. When Miss Pattilyn came for an unexpected visit two years ago, she was in tears saying that my father had died. I felt no remorse to my surprise but he was never there, he was always missing in the first place so I was angry at him instead. When the administrators of Fortis granted me leave to go home to attend my father's funeral which I refused made Andrew furious but I think he was mad not because I refused to come but he was more concern what the other Elites would think if the other son didn't pay respect to his own dead father. Miss Pattilyn was so disappointed of my decision then that she told me that my father loved my mother and he died because his heart couldn't take the pain of the loss. She conveyed that she thinks that my father never came to visit because I reminded him so much of her. We had the same long black hair and blue eyes that showed compassion and kindness that my father could not bear to look at me. She confessed that my mother was the most beautiful Duchess she had ever seen, everybody loved her even her servants and most especially my father and that they all wept when mother passed away. She told me not to blame my father for his indifference towards me and that if she knew I would act this way, she would have explained to me sooner, but how could Miss Pattilyn had known? She was only a servant to my father. Her words were just her thoughts of the reasons why my father acted that way so that it would appease me. We didn't have any proof how my father felt towards my mother or if he really died in despair of losing her, he took that story with him to his grave. So I moved on, never visiting the past except a few times when I remembered, what little memory I had of the loving moments with my mother when she was still with us. Those were the only time that I felt being truly loved, it was a brief and unclear moment but I knew and felt it and I treasured it the most.

A lot had happened to me over the years of growing up and Miss Pattilyn was always there. When I was old enough not to need a nanny, father made her in charge of our household which was an honor for a Delta, and she was ecstatic of the promotion. She was also one of those that never found a match in her younger years but that never stopped her from being happy, working diligently and loyal to the House of Bermule. Despite everything we've been through, I never thanked her. The only concept of what I have of what my mother was like before I was born was through her stories and so I decided that this was the right time to say my gratitude.

"Thank you Miss Pattilyn," I said.

She looked surprise but smiled, "Whatever for my Lord?"

"For everything, this might be the last visit," I explained.

She realized that what I meant of visit was our talks and she gave a huge grin that showed the signs of aging around her eyes.

"It has always been a pleasure my Lord. We would see more often now that you're coming home. You're free to visit me when you feel the need," she offered willingly.

I smiled back at her.

"So how's brother?" I asked to change the mood.

"Oh His Grace has been busy lately with the new Steel Plant he just opened yesterday," she responded as cheerfully as always, "I told him that you're coming home today and he looked delighted," she continued.

"I am sure he is," I remarked with sarcasm but Miss Pattilyn didn't notice it. She would have been more excited for me coming home than Andrew.

We arrived at the shuttle dock located in a nearby city and took our very own silver colored private air shuttle to Pinewood. When we finally arrived little had changed as I looked down from the window. Pinewood from the word itself had mostly trees, rivers, and green grass. Livestock were abundant here and the land had good soil for farming. Pinewood had many farmers, and acres of farms and lands owned by the House of Bermule and ruled by Andrew, the new Duke of Pinewood. Although our place was known for its farms, its recent main produced that had made us one of the wealthiest Dukedom was steel. We used lumber, which our lands were rich of, to make steel in our Steel Plants with modified machines that convert lumber to steel. Everything you see here to the horizon was all green like Fortis except for the mountains. A large river stretched for miles cutting through the woods where the wildlife of Pinewood would come for its fresh water. My home was here but I was still unfamiliar with the land, I have never been to the forest or to the rivers and looking down made me excited all of a sudden to seek an adventure and get lost in these woods.

Our shuttle started to descend, we had arrived at the Bermule Manor, a very large house that you could easily lose your way inside. The house has two parts, the east and the west wing. The west wing was solely for the Duke, the Duchess and their children while the east was for the guest rooms, offices, and where I would take residence. The Manor had a huge grand garden surrounding the grounds each with different plants and flowers of a variety of colors. Miss Pattilyn once told me that it was my mother who had these gardens built because she was fond of flowers. The gardens were still kept and cared for even after she was gone. The shuttle landed at a landing dock at the back part of the Manor grounds. We were greeted with footmen all clothed in silver with blue lining fine coats, the color of the House of Bermule, and its sigil was a tree. As I went down from the aircraft with Miss Pattilyn behind me, Mr. Thistle, our butler who wore his uniform a dark blue tail coat with silver lining came and slightly bowed to me saying, "Welcome home my Lord, the Duke of Pinewood wishes to see you in his private office."

"Thank you Mr. Thistle, it's nice to see you too," I replied grinning. I could hear Miss Pattilyn was trying to suppress a giggle.

"This way my Lord," Mr. Thistle directed with his hand while ignoring the comment I made.

Mr. Thistle, like Miss Pattilyn, had been with the family for a long time but he was loyal only to whoever had the title of Duke of Pinewood. He runs the entire household with Miss Pattilyn as his assistant, but often times they work together and usually they conflict on almost everything on how to run the household as what Miss Pattilyn shared with me before. Mr. Thistle was more strict, formal and uptight unlike Miss Pattilyn which became a problem for both of them before but they soon learned how to get along with each other running a very organized household for Bermule Manor.

Miss Pattilyn left us for her services were no longer

needed. I continued to follow Mr. Thistle to the Manor entering at the back entrance where guards in silver uniform were standing still at each side of the large door. While I was on my way to see my brother, the servants we passed by greeted me with a warm smile and a slight bow saying, "Welcome home my Lord." The housekeepers curtsied with beaming looks and giggles as I passed them, all happy to see me back.

"Back to work," Mr. Thistle commanded them as we went through the corridors where tall, and large glass windows with dark blue curtains tied elegantly at the sides brought the sunshine inside the manor. Everything was the same since the day I left, the white tiled walls and floors with silver accents on the wall moldings and a dark blue carpet that stretched at the center through the hallway. For a moment there, I was happy to be home. With all the friendly greetings and happy faces, it was good to be back.

We arrived at my brother's private office in the west wing. It was hard to think that this was my father's old office before he passed. Mr. Thistle knocked at the double entry door and waited for a respond.

"Yes?" I could hear my brother's voice from behind the door. Mr. Thistle entered and bowed, "Lord Curtis is here your Grace," he announced and he let me through.

"That will be all Mr. Thistle," Andrew dismissed him.

Mr. Thistle left us both in the room. At first I thought I would not recognize my brother, but I couldn't help it, he looked like a younger version of my father. The same sandy brown hair and dark brown eyes, but taller and he had a bigger built than my father or even me. He stood up from his chair behind his desk and came over to look at me closely. Then he sneered, unimpressed.

"Well, well, if it isn't my little ungrateful brother coming home to live under my roof," he said it mockingly while crossing his arms.

I stayed quiet trying to avoid any confrontation, it was my first day back home and I wasn't planning on spoiling my homecoming but seeing my brother, I had a bad feeling that I am at his mercy. He could kicked me out from the Manor if he wanted to, or do whatever he wants with me as long as he was the Duke of Pinewood.

As if he could read my mind, he sneered again and said, "Don't worry, you can stay here for now, but if you try to even annoy me or undermine or question my authority, I would throw you out in a heartbeat and strip you of any title," his tone suddenly became gravely serious while staring at me as if searching for any signs of defiance I may have, "Do you understand?" he continued in a low voice.

I suddenly became afraid, not of him, no, but of what was to become of me. We came from the same mother and father, yet it seemed we were more like strangers.

"Yes," I answered unwillingly trying to hide any signs of fear I had.

"Good, now come and give your brother a hug," he commanded.

I complied and we hugged for a brief moment without any emotions or care. A gesture only to validate the emptiness we had for each other.

CHAPTER 2: COASTAL CITY

ELAINE

I was getting ready for work, wearing my faded jeans, a white sleeveless top, and white sneakers, and I placed everything I needed inside my bag. I've only been accepted three months ago and I was already running late. I rummaged through my small room frantically searching for something to tie my hair with when I heard Mom calling my name from downstairs.

"Ellie!"

I didn't answer.

"Ellie," Mom called out louder this time.

I still didn't answer.

"Elaine Gertrue!!" she shouted.

"What?" I shouted back.

"You come down here and eat your breakfast or you'll miss your bus!" she ordered.

"Coming!"

I finally found my hair tie and fixed my hair back then came down stairs. When I went down to the kitchen, Dad was already at our small table eating his breakfast. He smiled when I entered and Mom was at the stove nearby preparing to serve my breakfast.

"Good morning Ellie," Dad greeted me happily.

I went over to him and kissed him on the cheek and greeted back sweetly, "Good morning Dad."

I sat on the chair near him while Mom placed a plate of eggs in front of me.

"Good morning dear, did you sleep well?" Mom asked affectionately.

"Yeah, it was fine," I responded nonchalantly.

Mom took a seat opposite from where I was and continued eating her breakfast.

"What's on the news Dad?"

Dad was drinking his coffee and looked at me while placing his newspaper aside.

"Oh the usual, news of the Empire," he reported.

"Have you read about the rebels? Those awful men trying to disrupt our peace," Mom spoke sounding disgusted.

"They're doing it probably for a good reason honey, and they are called Defiers," Dad explained but I could sense in his voice that he was teasing.

"Mr. Gertrue! Don't ever say it like that or it will get you in trouble, what would your fellow engineers at work say," Mom scolded.

"Don't worry dear, they usually don't say anything because they have their mates doing all the talking for them," Dad jokingly said with a large grin on his face.

I laughed but Mom didn't find it amusing.

"Ellie dear, could you slow down with your food?" Mom turned her attention back at me.

"Why? I am hungry. I came home late last night from work and was too tired to eat dinner," I defended.

"Well maybe you forgot, you recently turned twenty and who knows there will be a mail arriving soon bearing the name of your match," she reminded.

I almost forgot, I turned twenty a month ago making me eligible anytime soon, the thought of it made me nervous. I wasn't excited to get married not especially to someone who I had never met and we might never like each other.

"I don't want to get marry," I whined as if it would do me any good.

My Mom dropped her mouth in horror and was shocked at what I just said. Dad only sat there quietly listening.

"You know you can't refuse a match Ellie or you'll be in prison for life," she explained with a look of concern on her face, "And besides, marriage is good for you, it's a joining of resources and wealth that will help you and your soon to be match get by, and you'd want to have a child one day," she added.

I just rolled my eyes not convinced of her explanation.

"Who knows, you might love your mate someday," she continued.

"But," I hesitated, scared what their respond might be, "But what if I will never love my mate, not like you and Dad did. You two fell in love instantly when you met."

Mom was about to answer but Dad interrupted her, "We didn't fell in love right away."

I stared at him puzzled, waiting for an explanation.

"The moment I met your mother after I received the mail containing my match, I liked her and felt that I made a connection but I didn't love her, love came after," he described slowly, "Look Ellie, I will not try to pretend that everything is going to be alright because it is not. Marriage is work and I cannot assure you that you will love the man whoever will be your mate and," he paused then continued, "We honestly can't do anything about it. All you can do is live with it as best as you can. Of course I wish we could choose who our mate would be or we could refuse anyone who we think is not suitable for us or even have the freedom not to marry if we choose to but we can't. Just try to be happy my dear to whoever is chosen, and you may learn to love him after."

I sat in silence, pondering my Dad's words. I knew he

speaks the truth and he only wants what was best for me but it only made me angry at the System. The way things were, the obvious inequality and injustice especially to the lower stations. Being a Beta was not as bad as an Omega but there was still oppression and discrimination from the higher stations. Betas were only paid enough to get by but when the economy was low, the Betas and the Omegas were the ones that suffer the most while the Alphas and the Elites continue to live by in luxury without being affected. That was the reason I despised everything about them and what they represent. For me, they were all pretentious, self-absorb and corrupt beings that existed only to make us feel miserable. But I was not going to share these thoughts to my parents, they had work so hard for what they had earned. Dad was an engineer and Mom was an accountant, both were good and stable professions but when the Empire decides to increase our taxes and raised the cost of living, we had to give up a few things just so that we could make ends meet and afford food. If we ourselves had a hard time, how dire would it be for an Omega as well? We had neighbors who were Omegas who we sometimes help out if we had extra cash. Dad was always willing to help when they were in need. He always taught me that helping others was the most fulfilling feeling you could have in this lifetime, knowing that you helped changed the course of other people's lives by a simple act of kindness, and because of that, I always tried to live by my Father's words.

"Ellie, dear," Mom placed her hand on mine, "Be strong, I know when the time comes, you'll know what to do, and look at the bright side, when you turn fifty and you have no match yet then you'd be disqualified from the match and you'd get your wish," Mom tried to convince me on a positive note.

I could see in Dad's expression that he didn't know what to think of Mom's statement, if she was kidding about the last part or not but he gave her a loving smile anyway.

Most people would say that I looked like mom with her light brown hair, but I had my father's dark auburn wavy hair and green eyes. Although I resembled her, Mom and I would constantly argue about everything. She would always say to me that I was as stubborn as Dad. On the other hand, Dad was like a wise teacher to me. Teaching me the ways of life that the Yuvaika Institute could never do. My parents were lucky to find love, we knew some neighbors who couldn't stand around each other, and they just keep on bickering at one another and having a miserable life. I would be fortunate if I ever feel that instant connection, that moment when you lay your eyes on the mate you were to marry and you just knew that he was the one.

"I'm late, I better run," I declared standing up from my seat and took my bag without waiting for their respond.

"Bye Mon, bye Dad," I shouted as I went out the house.

"Bye Ellie," I heard my Dad say before I shut the door.

I was on the side of the street on a sunny morning. It was full of life which was not unusual on a typical day when everyone was preoccupied going to work. I was standing in front of our house when I took a deep breath of fresh air. I hated those kinds of conversations about the laws and marriage, it made me feel suffocated. I looked around the busy streets of our home and smiled at the familiar faces. The city got its name because it was located near the shores of the Great Ocean but you could barely see it from here. It was not the biggest city in the Empire but it was one of the most beautiful; with amazing scenic view of the ocean especially during sunset, and the weather here was mostly warm and sunny. People loved to come here mostly for relaxation, and the place was popular among the Alphas and the Elites but you would not see the likes of them in my neighborhood. Our place where the Betas and Omegas resides were full of small houses cramped side by side together that we could hear the voices of our neighbors sometimes if they spoke loudly and it was located in the southern part of Coastal City, away from the beaches and ocean. The neighborhood was clean and the vibrant colors of the houses made the place amusing to look at. This was home, I grew up here and learned to love it.

As I was about to leave, I realized that there was a man staring at me from across the street. He looked like he was younger than me or probably the same age. He was holding a broom, it seemed that he was sweeping the front of the bakery but stopped. He must be the new help Mrs. Dudley hired to help her out in her bakeshop. I stared back at him hoping that he would sense how rude it was, but he just hesitantly smiled at me with his gleaming dark blue eyes. It was then that I immediately walked away ignoring him. It was not the first time that I caught men taking a short glimpsed at me and I always find it very uncomfortable.

    I almost missed my bus when I arrived. The ride would take us to the northern part of the city where everything was near the ocean, and the streets were wide in dark asphalt. This was where all the soaring glass buildings, and expensive hotels, and elegant private apartments of the Elites were built. This district was the main commercial area of Coastal City full of different people going about their own business. From my stop, I had to walk where the Animal Clinic was for about twenty minutes but I did not mind the distance, the weather was always warm in Coast City except when there were the occasional ocean storms that it pours nonstop.

I got to work just in time. I entered the locker room to change to my working coat.

"Hi Ellie," a woman's voice greeted me. I turned around from my locker to see who it was.

"Hi Sarah," I smiled. Sarah and I worked together; she had been working here longer than I have. When I started, she was the first to become my friend with her sweet and cheerful soul that it was easy to be her friend.

"Getting ready for another late night?" I teased.

Sarah let out a soft laugh, "Please I can't handle two nights in a row."

"I bet you can," I encouraged her with a smile.

"I'm not as strong as you are," she responded, "and besides, I have a child to take care of."

I giggled then we both wore our white coat and went inside to start working. As we entered the room, a friendly face welcomed us.

"Aaahh.. Good morning! My super duos are finally here. Would you mind if you two could take a look at this dog doctors?"

We smiled and greeted in unison, "Good morning Doctor Cook."

Doctor Cook was the head of the Animal Clinic. He had been working here all his life and he seems happy and contented to be doing so.

"What do we have here?" I asked as I went over the examining table. It was a small dog with long yellow golden hair with eyes like black buttons looking at me happily.

"The owners that brought her here complained that she hasn't been eating recently," Doctor Cook explained.

"Oh she is so cute, what's her name?" Sarah inquired holding the dog on her arms while it wagged its tail.

"Her name is..." Doctor Cook looked over the information sheet, "Cotton."

"Such a nice name," Sarah declared sweetly, "Don't worry Cotton, I'll do some test to see if you're alright."

"Uuuh.. actually, I was hoping Ellie would do that," Doctor Cook interjected.

Sarah looked confused.

"I need you to look at another dog Sarah at Richmond Apartments, one owned by Lady Georgina," He requested.

The Coastal City Animal Clinic takes in any type of animals, pets or livestock. Most of the owners were from the Alphas and the Elites, and sometimes the Betas if they can afford them. So when an Elite calls for our services, they were given the utmost priority and the best. Second only to Doctor Cook, Sarah was the best we had at the clinic especially with small pets. It was an honor to be at service to an Elite, it helps boost the reputation but I did not envy her for that, the Elites treat their pets with more respect than us from what I heard, but nobody had to worry about that when it came to Sarah, she was favored by the Elites for her remarkable skills with pets and her sweet nature so naturally they would request for her whenever they had problems with their pets.

"Sure," she agreed cheerfully.

"I'll take her," I offered and took Cotton to be examined.

Sarah left for Richmond Apartment a while after. The day went on the Animal Clinic with nothing out of the ordinary. Not much excitement happens here in the clinic except for the emergencies that seldom occur like last night but I loved it here, I felt that this was where I belonged. At a young age, we were tested on what career we would be good at and I passed every test and training to become an animal doctor and my love for animals helped a lot too. Only a few pets came by the clinic today so we spent most of our time taking care of those who were here to be hospitalized, and if we had a spare time, we played and bond with the pets that were well enough. I enjoyed spending time with them because some lack care and attention; some owners owned pets just so they can have one even though they were rarely home to take care of them. Like Cotton for instance, the test result came in and found nothing wrong with her. She was probably just depressed that she didn't had the appetite to eat but she was faring better when I took her for a walk and played with her. She ate the food I fed her and gave her gentle strokes on her back as she started to fall asleep. Her owner, an Alpha, will be here soon to pick her up and I pity Cotton when she goes back home, she'll be sad all over again. I wish I could take her home with me instead but I cannot afford to.

Sarah came back from her trip from Richmond. She shared her stories on how adorable Lady Georgina's dog was and how huge was her apartment. She was ecstatic that the Lady let her stayed to have lunch there. Of course she didn't dine with the Lady but she was happy all the same that she had the chance to try such expensive dishes. She went on and on about her experiences until it was time to get ready to go home. I said my goodbyes to Sarah and the staff then I took the bus home, there was still daylight and I was glad I get to go home early. I rode in silence like the rest of the passengers. There was an old lady sitting next to me near the aisle. She looked tired but contented with her time on the bus maybe eager to finally go home like me. There was mother and her son seated in front, she was whispering something in his ear and it made him giggle. They looked happy together but it would be painful when they would spend their life apart when he would have to go to Fortis Institute. Parents were allowed to visit but for Omegas, Deltas and Betas, it would be costly and they would have to apply for leave from their job. Mom and Dad visited me once or twice a month or sometimes every other month; there were times when they could not visit together when one of them could not leave work. It was hard for them and hard for me too but I was grateful for their sacrifices, and I try not to disappoint them because of that.

    The bus reached our stop and I was walking on my way home. The streets were not as busy as this morning anymore. I took my time, enjoying the daylight before it goes dark. I passed little shops and bigger stores, not all Betas earned the same and in the Empire, the Beta or Omega who earned more paid more taxes so it would be hard to become wealthy for a Beta or Omega. I was approaching my house and I noticed again the man outside the bakery. He was closing the bakeshop then he saw me and gave me a huge smile. I ignored him yet again and kept my head down as I was entering the house.

    "Ellie you're back, how was work today?" Mom asked cheerfully.

"It was fine, nothing special."

"Good then you could help me set up for dinner."

"Sure Mom."

I prepared the dining table while Mom was cooking dinner. It was getting dark outside as we were about to finish.

"I think your dad is running late," Mom stated.

Just as we were about to sit down, Dad entered the house.

"Sorry I'm late, busy day at work," he apologized while he placed his bag on the couch and came to the kitchen and took a seat at the dining table with us.

"It's okay dear, how was your day?" Mom asked.

"Exhausting! But I want to hear more how my two favorite girls' day was."

Mom was now talking nonstop about her day at work while I listened absent mindedly. I was thankful that they didn't bring up the conversation we had this morning, since I wasn't in the mood for it.

We finished our dinner and I went upstairs to my room. I was lying in my small bed wasting my time wondering when I will receive a mail with my match's name on it. The thought made me nervous then it came across that what if my match would be like the man from the bakery store? I pondered on the idea for a while. I honestly wouldn't mind though. I thought he was handsome especially his smile and the way his blue eyes glows in the light like the ocean and his blonde hair that shines like gold. He would probably make a good mate but what was I thinking? Of course we cannot be together, it was never a choice and besides there was no chance for a Beta to be matched with an Omega. People who tried to go against the law and the system by secretly having a relationship with others who were not matched together were sent to prison. Most of them were caught because someone reported, even by suspicion you can be reported, then the Protectors would be on to you or interrogate you and your invalid partner. I overheard once about a year ago from my parents that a close friend of theirs fell in love with his fellow worker and the woman felt the same way about him. The woman was married but was not fond of her match. My parents didn't report them, they couldn't bear the thought that they would have to die for the crime they had committed. However, they did warn them to exercise caution but eventually someone did report them, and no one knew who. I heard dad told mom that they were arrested, interrogated, and never heard from again. The match that the woman left behind never remarried for no one was ever allowed to remarry however manner they lose their mates. You only get matched once in your lifetime. I let out a deep breath; all this nonsense thoughts got me tired when I knew there was no possibility so there was no point on acting on it.

 The next day, I left the house early for work. I said my goodbyes to mom and dad and went out the door. The morning had a clear blue sky and sunshine. I was about to go on my way to the bus stop when I noticed the man again across the street. He was opening the bakery, and then he saw me and gave a warm smile. For some reason, maybe because of the thrill or stupidity, I smiled back, then left as quickly as I could realizing what a mistake that was. At the corner of my eye, I could see his expression turned from surprise to ecstatic while scratching the back of his head. I was riding the bus when I told myself that it was only a friendly smile and nothing more.

There was no law against making new friends. Get a hold of yourself Ellie! I would never hurt mom and dad so I needed to be careful not to send the wrong impression.

I arrived at the Animal Clinic. Sarah wasn't in yet so it meant that I was early. I helped the animal attendants with their morning feeding and care for the animals that stayed in the clinic while waiting for my shift to start. I was feeding a little kitten when Dr. Cook approached me with a worried look on his face.

"Oh hi Dr. Cook, what's up?" I greeted.

"Ellie, Sarah left a message that she can't come for work today," Dr. Cook anxiously said.

"Is everything alright? Did she said why?" I asked with concern.

"Her son has the cold and she needs to take him to the doctor to have him check."

"That's awful, I hope he will be okay."

It was funny that our pioneers had mastered the science of conception through blood and gene modification but they did not bother to give us the immunity from the common cold. I guessed despite all their knowledge, they themselves were not perfect to play gods.

"I hope so too. Anyway, I came here to ask if you could do her rounds while she's not here Ellie," Dr. Cook requested with a pleading look.

"Sure it's not a problem Dr. Cook," I offered willingly.

"Uumm.. I was also thinking of her follow up services," he hesitated.

"What do you mean?"

"Sarah had a follow up schedule with Lady Georgina's dog this morning at Richmond Apartment and since she's not here," he reluctantly implied.

"You want me to go to Richmond?"

Dr. Cook had a pleading smile, "Please Ellie, I have no one and you know we can never cancel or postpone an appointment with an Elite. You're one of the best I've got."

"Wouldn't she be expecting Sarah?" I was trying to get myself out of this.

"Well yes but you could explain to her why Sarah can't come," he suggested eagerly.

"Why don't you go instead doctor? You're the best here."

"I can't leave the clinic Ellie and you know that," he was begging.

Dr. Cook knew I was not fond of servicing the Elites but I cannot refuse him, he was the chief and the boss even though what he said sounded more like a request.

"Fine," I surrendered, "But don't be surprised if you don't hear again from Lady Georgina after this."

He was thrilled that I agreed, "Thank you, thank you, I'm sure you'd be fine."

I left the clinic that morning to catch the bus going to Richmond. I brought the medicine bag along and Dr. Cook told me the necessary details that I needed to know about Lady Georgina's dog. The apartment was near the ocean where most of the expensive hotels and apartments were which was the lavish part of the city. It took me two bus rides to get there. I wasn't excited; I dreaded arriving there that I hoped my bus took the wrong turn. The bus stopped near the apartment. The doorman opened the double door as I was about to enter. I approached the man behind the reception desk and told him who I was, why I was there and who I intended to visit. The man checked his list and nodded, meaning I was expected since Dr. Cook made the necessary phone call early this morning. He rang for the footman to assist and guide me to Lady Georgina's floor. I followed the footman wearing a fancy long red coat who was willing enough to accompany me. Everything inside the building had a classic feel to it. There were paintings and sculpture that I imagined could feed a lot of families if sold. We rode an elevator made entirely of glass and it ascended to the top floors. We finally arrived and the lobby was exquisite made out of gold and marble and there was a large fountain in the middle. I had never seen such a magnificent room, I was both impressed and in awe. A butler approached us and the footman informed him who I was.

"This way please," the butler said with such courteous manner and motioned me to follow him.

We went through the hallway, passing rooms which were as glorious as the next. We stopped at a room at the end of the hallway and the butler asked me to wait here as he entered first to announce my arrival. Once the Lady consented, the butler led me inside the room and left. I felt terrified all of a sudden, I did not know what to expect. There seated in a huge extravagant couch in the middle of the room was a woman with a black hair fixed into a bun. She was wearing a Lady's dress, made with elegant and expensive fabric of red with pattern designs of black and gold, the dress had a three quarter length sleeves, and a wide skirt that was until the ankles. These dresses were only made for the Lady's in the Elites to wear. A small white dog was lying on her lap which stared when I entered. I could sense that this Lady was born from a very wealthy and proud family by just the look of her and how she carried herself. I did not know what to do so I hesitantly curtsied; it was the only thing I could think of that was appropriate. The dog started barking, it had this annoying little bark but the Lady was not bothered.

"I thought the girl who came yesterday was supposed to be here," she declared with a stern and regal demeanor, her words came slowly and calmly and without the sound of care. She did not even look at me when she spoke; she just stared down at her dog while she gently stroke its hair.

I felt nervous, searching for the proper words to respond, "Apologies my Lady, but Sarah couldn't come in today because of a family emergency she needed to attend to," I stammered, I could feel myself sweating even though the room was cold.

Did I say it the proper way? I did not know how to act or what to say to them, she was the very first Elite I had talked to and met up close.

Lady Georgina did not move or react to anything I just said. She remained unaffected and bored. She let out a deep sigh and finally looked at me and said, "And here I am asking for your services and you people couldn't even send the very best," she had a look of disappointment in her while she shook her head, "Very well, you will have to do," she conceded like she did not had a choice. I was uncertain at first then I came close enough to where she was seated and placed the medicine bag on the floor.

"May I?" I asked in a most polite way I could muster.

The Lady did not answer so I assumed it was okay, I tried to gently pat and take the small dog away from her but it suddenly let out a loud yelp and almost bit me; but instead of Lady Georgina showing concern, she slapped the top of my hand.

"What are you doing?!" she scolded.

"I was just trying to..." I tried to explain but she immediately interrupted, "You fool! Little Chester doesn't want to be touched by anyone, how dare you even tried," she yelled.

I stared at her in disbelief as if it was my fault. How was I going to treat the dog without going near it? And if she said sooner that little Chester was not friendly to strangers then we could have avoided all this. I had respect for Lady Georgina but she was starting to get on my nerves.

"I knew this would happen, I can't believe they sent me someone so incompetent," she kept on ranting, only this time her face turned red and enraged that she started hyperventilating.

I wonder how Sarah handled this, did Chester tried to bite her as well? I did not think Chester was harmful but Lady Georgina was. If there was someone who needs training, it was her. So I tried to calm her down and ignore her insults, attempting to be on top of the situation.

"Lady Georgina," I said as calm as possible, "I need you to let me hold Chester for a while so that I can administer the needed medication. I know I am not the top choice but believe me I am more than competent enough to know the difference between genuine concern and excessiveness. In the meantime, I am the best of what you've got for Chester or with all due respect I could leave and stop wasting your time, my Lady," I tried to smile hoping I did not sound mean.

Lady Georgina opened her mouth in disbelief. This must be the first time someone was blunt enough to talk to her like that, then she closed her mouth tight and was speechless. She stared at me then straightened her clothes and composed herself trying to regain her dignity. She then handed me Chester and I took him in my arms. Chester suddenly became calmed as if he too was shocked at what he heard. I placed Chester on my lap as I sat on the floor and took the medication out from the bag. I gave him the shot and he did not move at all so I commended him, "Good boy Chester." He wagged his tail when I gave him a dog treat after. I returned Chester to Lady Georgina who accepted him and give him a kiss and a pat. I placed everything back in the bag and was preparing to leave. I felt suddenly bad for what I said to her. I should had known better and I should not have let my temper get the best of me. I looked at her once more and gave her a tight smile hoping she would consider it as a how sorry I was sign. I was about to exit the room when Lady Georgina out of nowhere said to me, "You know you're different," she paused and I stopped at the door not turning back to face her in fear that she might say something insulting again.

"Someday it is going to get you in trouble.... or might get you far in life," she continued in a softer tone. I turned around to face her, there was no hate on her face, and she was solemn as she stared back at me. I nodded silently in respond then left the room hoping that I would never return to this place again.

    I was looking forward to going home today, I did not know why, probably because of the stressful morning I had. I was walking on my usual route and as I was nearing my house, I saw the man from across the street again. I swear I think he waits for me whenever I go out the house or when I come home. He saw me coming and he was beaming while waving. I walked faster and glanced at him and I gave a little smile so not to seem rude then I ran to the door like I was afraid of him. I left my things at the living room and I noticed mom was already at the kitchen preparing our dinner. I was about to help her but I heard a knocked at the door.

"I'll get it," I yelled.

"Okay honey," mom responded.

I opened the door and there he was, the man from across the street holding something wrapped in a white clean cloth. I was surprised when I saw him, not only because how good he looked up close but also that he was there at my doorstep which was the very last place I wanted him to be.

He was smiling broadly then laughed a little then I realized that he was laughing at my surprised expression. I closed my mouth that I did not even realize were opened. I tried to compose myself trying not to feel awkward then I cleared my throat, "May I help you?"

He kept on smiling that made his eyes twinkle more and I could feel myself losing control, excited and afraid at the same time. For the first time in my life I felt alive. It was like, before this moment, everything was a blur, as if a cloud was in front of me all this time but it was finally lifted and I saw clearly every details and I did not know why his face was the center of it all but I could not resist staring.

"I came to deliver this loaf of bread for Mrs. Gertrue," he replied happily.

For some reason, I couldn't comprehend the words he said so it took me a minute to gather my thoughts and I was about to say something when mom came over.

"Ellie, what are you doing just standing there?" mom was looking at me annoyed.

"Please tell Mrs. Dudley thank you for this fresh bread," she said gratefully while taking the loaf of bread from him.

"I will Mrs. Gertrue," he complied willingly.

Mom left us and I remained at the door speechless. I had no idea what was I waiting for so to break the embarrassing pause, I just said, "Thank you," and I slowly closed the door but halfway through, he said in the most gentle way, "You're welcome. See you tomorrow?"

"Huh?" I was confused what he meant by that.

He chuckled, "Tomorrow on your way to work," he explained.

"Oh!" it was all I could muster as I felt myself blushing and feeling foolish. I smiled at him and shut the door and I leaned on it and felt completely embarrassed by what just happened.

"Aaargh.. kill me now," I told myself while I buried my face in my hands. I can't walk out there tomorrow with him across the street. Maybe if I go to work early I wouldn't see him. I let out a deep breath, feeling exhausted and defeated. I stayed by the door for a while. Was this what it felt like to have feelings for someone? The sensation that was discouraged by the law unless you were matched to each other; but it was hard to live without acting on it or even not having the choice to try. Was this what the lawbreakers felt? The emotions that they felt for each other that they were willing to risk their freedom or even their lives for it? To be free but not having the one thing you ever wanted; or risk everything just to spend those moments in hiding with the one you love. In the end though, we were all prisoners.

CHAPTER 3: HOMECOMING

CURTIS

It felt good finally spending some time outside the manor. It has been two weeks since my arrival at Pinewood and I had been longing to explore the land just to have an excuse to leave the house. Horseback riding was a good idea especially in the early morning, and it felt comfortable wearing my Lord's clothes for a change and not the uniform from the Institute. A short black frockcoat and a white collared shirt and gray vest underneath, beige pants tucked in on my long leather dark brown boots, and a black buckle was better in my opinion. The air was cooler as it hit my face when my black stallion galloped through the green meadow on a cloudy day. Although Mr. Witherson, who cared for our horses, kept on discouraging me from riding today especially when the grounds were wet from the rains the other day. I understood his concerns because no one spoke about it freely but I shared the same fond for horses with my mother and it was a day like this that led to the accident that caused my mother's untimely death while on horseback riding. I finally persuaded Mr. Witherson that it was safe and told him that I was good with horses which he already knew. He wanted us to wait for the ground to be dry enough but I couldn't wait and besides, the weather in Pinewood was so unpredictable that it was either rainy or sunny or sometimes both on the same day. I could hear the mud squished under the hooves of my horse as I slowed down to a trot when we approached the woods. Peter, my escort, was having a hard time catching up with his horse which had less speed compared to my larger and faster stallion. He looked pleased when I slowed down when he finally caught up. Peter was scrawny built and was probably two or three years older than me. I would bet that he was one of Andrew's errand boy, an Omega that he did not needed anymore then assigned him to me. I was not complaining though, Peter was hard working, obedient and never complained. He never spoke unless spoken to, I am not sure if it was because he feared me or was just shy. He was also useful because he knew the people and the land making him an excellent guide.

We rode side by side when we entered the forest. The trees here were colossal and their roots overlapped one on top of the other. The smell of the wet grass and leaves was stronger here and you could hear the rustling branches swaying against each other when the wind blew hard. I was looking around and thought to myself that you could get lost here despite the narrow path that goes through these woods.

"How much farther?" I asked Peter.

"A little farther my Lord, as long as we stick to the path, we'll be out in no time," he replied.

"What's beyond these woods?"

"One of the small farming village my Lord, we could take a rest there."

"Good," I responded contented with the idea.

I reined my horse to a stop and Peter did the same with his. I heard something rustled nearby then under the dead leaves a little gray rabbit emerged and went its way back to the woods when it realized that it was not alone.

"Remind me the name of this forest?"

"Greendale, my Lord," Peter answered eagerly, "I

should give caution my Lord. These woods are dangerous at night, it is when the wolves come out and hunt," he warned me.

I nodded, "And this is the fastest way?"

"Yes my Lord but I highly dissuade you to take this path. Few people take this road, most of them will take the long way around Greendale forest," he declared trying to convince me.

"Duly noted."

It was not Peter's plan to take this road when we started this journey but I insisted we go through here for a shorter route. He was not happy about it but he did not have a choice. Greendale was the biggest and thickest forest in Pinewood. Miss Pattilyn used to tell me stories when I was a child about this forest and the many haunting creatures that lurks in it to scare me. It did not look terrifying during the day though but I would not risk going through here at night.

We rode in silence until we reached the other end of the forest. The sun finally shone, and it was passed midday.

"Are we near the village?" I asked impatiently.

"Not far my Lord, just straight ahead."

I motioned my horse to gallop towards the nearest village. Peter followed from behind. We arrived not long after. The farm fields were stretched around the village. People stopped what they were doing on the fields to watch us as we slowly passed by. There were whispers and when they recognized who I was they bowed. Some had a welcoming smile while some looked curious.

"May I lead the way my Lord?" Peter asked.

I nodded giving him my consent. He rode ahead of me and I followed. We passed some more fields and houses until we reached the village and came upon a small white house and it had wooden fences and a small garden on the front yard. A man came out of the house grinning and eager to welcome when he saw us got off from our horses outside his home. He had dark black hair and a few grays, and he was not tall but stocky built, and had a jolly smile.

"Welcome my Lord, we weren't expecting to see you here," he greeted us with a cheerful tone.

"My Lord, may I present Mr. James Conolly, in charge of the Eastwood First Village," Peter introduced him with utmost respect.

Mr. Conolly bowed and spoke very politely and happily, "My Lord, may I offer my humble home to be at your disposal."

I smiled at him and replied, "You are most kind Mr. Conolly, if it isn't any trouble, I would be honored to."

"No trouble My Lord, please come," he motioned us to follow him.

We were at the doorstep when I noticed there were two women both with long blonde hair waiting.

"Aaah.. My Lord, may I present my mate and my daughter Hannah."

They curtsied after the introduction with their lovely smiles.

"Good afternoon, I am very sorry to interrupt on this lovely day," I said in a most apologetic manner.

I saw Hannah gazing at me so I looked at her and gave her a warm smile. She giggled and I saw her face turned to red.

"You're not interrupting my Lord, please come in, forgive our small house," Mrs. Conolly opened the door for us to let us through.

The house made out entirely of wood was not a manor

but it had a homey atmosphere inside. Everything was pleasant and warm, and you could tell that it was a happy place. Mr. Conolly ushered us to the dining area which was also the kitchen. The table was set which looked like they were about to have their lunch before we interrupted them. Mrs. Conolly and Hannah hurriedly set two extra plates for us, one at the head of the table and the other on the left side while they moved their own plates to give space.

"I am really sorry once again, it seems that we were intruding while you were having your lunch," I expressed my regret.

"Oh no my Lord, we are truly happy and honored to have you dine with us today, it is not everyday we have visitors around especially from a Lord of the House of Bermule," Mr. Conolly beamed, "and besides, I should be the one asking for forgiveness my Lord, as you can see we only prepared such a decent meal. If we knew you were coming, we could have prepared a feast for you my Lord," he continued sounding worried.

I examined the table, "Is this all grown from here? And cooked by your lovely mate?" I asked.

"Yes my Lord," Mr. Conolly replied proudly and cheerfully while glancing lovingly at his mate.

I looked at him and said, "Then I look forward to this feast, nothing can stop me from eating the produce grown on the lands of Pinewood."

Mr. Conolly's was elated as he guided me to have a seat at the head of the table while he took the right seat and Peter on the left with Hannah beside him, Mrs. Conolly took the seat beside Mr. Conolly.

The table became alive, Mr. Conolly was chatting away about what it was like in the village while we passed around the food. This was my first in such a setting; it was completely new to me but in a very pleasant way. There were beans, carrots, and potatoes boiled and mixed and flavored. A loaf of bread which I could see was made from scratch by Hannah as Mr. Conolly boasted of it. An entire chicken from their barn was roasted by Mrs. Conolly herself. Everything smelled good and tasted delicious. For dessert, Mrs. Conolly placed her lemon pie on the table which she used the lemons from her garden that she planted herself and made it taste heavenly. I was full after the meal and I have never been happier since the day I arrived that I get to experienced such homemade food carefully prepared with love. These were not like the extravagant food served at the manor but this was for me far more superior.

"Mrs. Conolly, your mate is a very lucky man to come home everyday to eat such delicious meal," I complimented.

Mrs. Conolly was beaming and humbly replied, "Thank you my Lord, I am so pleased you like my cooking, it means a great deal."

"And a compliment to Hannah, who knew such delicate hands could knead such a soft and tasty bread," I continued acknowledging her skills and she shyly smiled.

After lunch, Mrs. Conolly served us coffee while Hannah took away the plates to be washed.

"Would you like to take our coffee my Lord in the living room?" Mr. Conolly humbly suggested.

"Certainly," I complied happily.

We brought our coffee to the other room and sat at the comfortable cushions and drank our coffee.

"So Mr. Conolly, how's the harvest this time of year?" I

spoke first.

"Couldn't be better my Lord, the land is still rich and the rainy season is coming which is good for the crops. Let's just hope there will be no storms," he responded.

"Let's hope not," I concurred, "Any problems you encountered so far?" I added.

Mr. Conolly suddenly became reluctant to answer. He cleared his throat and finally spoke, "Well, my Lord, there's no problem that we can't handle," he grinned unconvincingly. I sense that he was not completely telling the truth and he did a poor job of hiding it.

I looked down at my cup and took a sip, placed it on the coffee table in front of me, and looked at Mr. Conolly in the eye. I could see that he was getting uncomfortable.

"It's okay, you can tell me," I assured him.

Mr. Conolly had a surprised look on his face and glanced at Peter unsure of me. He became uneasy on his seat but eventually he spoke, "Well, since you asked my Lord," he hesitated again then continued, "We're having problems with our harvest lately, we're having a hard time completing the quota with the lack of manpower and equipment."

"Lack of manpower?" I repeated.

"Yes, my Lord, most of the able men and women have been recently working at the Steel Plants rather than on the farms," he explained.

"Go on," I urged him to continue, "Is it because of the higher pay at the Steel Plants?"

Mr. Conolly paused before answering, "Not exactly my Lord," he shifted on his seat and his brows were starting to sweat.

"What then?"

Mr. Conolly didn't speak.

I was confused, "You mean some of them are forced to work at the Plants? But I thought people preferred to work there?" I presumed.

"Oh yes my Lord, some probably preferred to work there but some...." Mr. Conolly resisted but finally gave in, "some don't because of the working conditions...."

I frowned, thinking that our working conditions at the Plant were always safe and clean so I did not completely understand his meaning why this was a problem.

"I'll make inquiries about that, in the meantime, you could request for more equipment to help in the harvest to compensate for the lack of manpower," I suggested.

"We did my Lord but it never came," he shook his head, "We make a living out of our farms my Lord and a large portion of it is given to the Dukedom as payment for the lands that belongs to the Duke. If we fail to meet the quota, the Duke will strip us out from our farms and our homes and we have nowhere else to go if that happened," he continued looking very upset.

I felt sympathy for Mr. Conolly and the villagers. I could see that the men and women here were working hard to keep their farms and homes, and I wanted to help.

"Do not worry Mr. Conolly, I'll speak with the Duke about this personally, and we'll find a way to help you with your farms," I promised with a reassuring tone.

He suddenly became his cheerful self again after I told him that, "Oh thank you my Lord, we will be forever grateful to you."

"Well, we better get going. We still have a long way to go," I smiled as I took our leave.

"Of course my Lord," Mr. Conolly agreed as he stood up and accompanied us to the door. Peter went out first in a hurry to prepare our horses. I stood at the doorway and held out my hand to Mr. Conolly, then he accepted and shook it, "Thank you again Mr. Conolly, I had a marvelous time with you and your family in your lovely home," I stated with gratitude.

"Our home is your home my Lord, you are always welcome here. Do come see us again," he offered happily.

I nodded and smiled, "I'll certainly do that."

I waved my goodbyes to Mrs. Conolly and Hannah and they waved back smiling. I walked across the small front yard towards Peter where he was waiting with the horses. He held the bridle as I climbed up the saddle then he rode his. I gave one last look at Mr. Conolly and his family then we left. We passed again the houses and the fields on our way out of the village. The villagers bowed and some waved as we rode away.

"Where to next my Lord?" Peter asked respectfully.

"Take me to one of the Steel Plants Peter," I requested.

"There's one here at Eastwood my Lord and there's Westwood where most of the Plants are," he informed.

"Westwood then," I decided.

We rode with Peter leading the way, traveling through smaller farms and villages, and trees. I took our time enjoying the scenery. The sun was still up but the cool wind was blowing, and the birds were singing like they were grateful for the beautiful day. We stopped on a hilltop and Peter nodded his head towards a place not far.

"That's Moors, the town between the borders of Eastwood and Westwood my Lord, shall we take a look?"

"Sounds like a good idea," I declared.

We rode forward and arrived at Moors town. It was full of people from all over, mostly farmers, merchants and steel workers. It was a lively place where some came to sell or to buy, and some came just to have a good time. There were market stalls, bars, shops, and inns all cramped inside this small town. Nobody seemed to know who I was which was a relief. We left our horses at the town stable and continued on foot. We entered a bar and ordered a cold beer. We sat at our table at the far end of the room minding our business. I was watching the people come and go the crowded bar when I noticed a man with a short white hair wearing a leather black coat sitting alone from across the room staring at me.

"Peter, there's a man staring at our direction behind you. Do you recognize him?" I asked in a low voice.

Peter who sat opposite me slowly turned around trying not to look conspicuous. After he saw him, he faced me and shook his head, "No my Lord."

The man was still watching us, drank all his beer and stared directly at me one more time then stood up and left the bar. I found his actions odd, maybe he recognized me and chose not to acknowledge it but it does not matter since he was gone anyway.

Peter suddenly interrupted while I was with my thoughts, "My Lord it's getting late I suggest that we stay at the inn for the night before we proceed to Westwood tomorrow."

"No, I was thinking of staying somewhere else," I declined his proposal.

He looked puzzled, then asked, "Where my Lord?"

I took a drink from my cup before I answered, "Let's camp outside for the night."

It was clear that Peter was not enthusiastic of the idea, "I would not recommend that my Lord, it could be dangerous," he warned.

"Oh come on, you and I both know that travelers often sleep and hunt outdoors, and I am sure you have tried it without running into trouble."

"Yes my Lord but with all due respect, I am not the Lord of Pinewood," he explained trying to dissuade me.

I grinned at his comment then added, "No you're not but that doesn't make me any less entitled to camp outside, and besides, you know the land, I trust you know the safest places."

Peter sighed, "As you wish my Lord, but we need to make preparations first."

"Sure, we will buy the necessary things that you say we need," I agreed.

"And if we are going to sleep outside my Lord, the best place and the safest would be by the river," he stated with authority this time.

I smiled at his firm attitude, "It's a deal then."

We left the bar and bought the necessary supplies we needed for the camp. I bought two bows and arrows for the hunt from one of the market stalls and gave one to Peter. The bows looked good made from strong wood from the trees of Pinewood. I had experience in using one of these back at Fortis in an archery class. We then returned to the stables and paid the stable keeper after he retrieved our horses, and we rode out of town before it went dark.

The river was not that wide but it stretched for miles and it even passed near the manor; It was not so deep and the current was not strong that you could cross it without any trouble. We arrived at the nearest river bank and made camp. We let the horses graze while we gathered for woods to build a fire later. I was checking the bow I bought, trying to feel the weight of it and placed an arrow on the bow string.

"Have you ever shot one my Lord?" Peter asked while

holding his own bow.

I shot an arrow at a nearby tree, and it landed at the center of the trunk.

Peter grinned.

"I guess I still know how to use one of this but I haven't tried hunting before," I confessed.

"It's easy my Lord, just aim the arrow straight forward," he encouraged.

"Shall we?" I proceeded into the woods with Peter right behind with our bows on hand and the arrows on our back. We walked slowly careful not to scare any creature worth hunting. Sure enough a moment later, Peter spotted a rabbit hiding in the bushes. The brown rabbit was slowly walking around searching for food. We stood our ground and made sure not to make any sudden movements. I placed an arrow on the string and stretched the bow aiming it at the unaware rabbit, then I released, it pierced right through its body.

"Nice shot my Lord," Peter complimented smiling at my triumph.

"Lucky shot," I chuckled.

I hunted two rabbits and I gave Peter a shot at the third. The sun was almost setting so we decided to hunt our last one. We were already deeper into the woods when Peter suddenly tapped my shoulder as we were slowly walking. I looked at him and he silently gestured me to crouch down with him which I obliged. We were hidden behind tall grasses and Peter pointed at the right side just behind a tree where a doe suddenly emerged. She was magnificent; it was the first one I saw up close. The doe moved her head around curious of the surroundings and nibbling at some grasses, and slowly moving gracefully towards us.

"Aim near the chest my Lord," Peter whispered.

I silently mounted an arrow and pulled the string of the bow while kneeling. As I took aim, the doe saw me but instead of running away, she stared back at me. There was a look of innocence and trust in its eyes and it didn't seem to regard me as a threat. I was still aiming the arrow but I didn't had the heart to release it.

"Is everything alright my Lord?" Peter whispered with a hint of concern.

I aimed the bow down and relaxed the string.

"Nothing, I was just thinking we have enough for today," I explained.

Peter nodded and did not say anything.

We went back to camp. I started the fire while Peter skinned and cleaned the rabbits. He showed me how to do it and how to cook it. Night was upon us when we finished eating. The fire was burning bright in the dark and I lay on the blanket gazing at the stars fascinated on how magnificent they were. Everything was quiet and peaceful save the crackling sound of the burning wood. I never felt so relaxed and I couldn't help wondering what it would be like to spend every night like this under the stars, with no manor or titles and the responsibilities that comes with it. Then I looked at Peter, who was sitting across from me carving the end of a wood stick with his knife.

"How often do you do this Peter? Spending the night outside," I asked intrigued.

He was surprised by my question but he willingly replied, "When I am home my Lord. My dad and I would camp outside when we go hunting."

"That's nice, your dad taught you how to hunt?"

He nodded, "Since I was a child my Lord."

"Where are you from?"

"Eastwood my Lord."

"Oh, were we near your home? We could have paid a visit if I knew."

"It's okay my Lord, no need to, my home is out of the way from our route."

There was silence.

"Did you grew up on a farm?" I continued.

"Yes my Lord, almost the same as the First Village."

"So you know Mr. Conolly?"

"Yes my Lord, my father and Mr. Conolly had been trading for a long time, I passed by their village every time I have a chance to go home."

I stared at the stars once again and imagined what it must be like for Peter traveling home and going through the meadows and woods, and spending the night like this.

"Are you and your father close?" for some reason I didn't know why I asked that personal question. I glanced at his direction and he stopped what he was doing and with the light from the fire on his face, I could see the surprised and hesitant expression. I would understand if he refused to answer; Omegas were not used to Elites asking very personal questions.

Peter then continued carving the wood and smiled, "Yes my Lord, I couldn't ask for a better father," he said with pride.

I grinned back, I was happy for him. I continued staring at the stars without saying another word. Peter was lucky to have a close relationship with his father, I somewhat envy him and it made me sad that I would never know what it would be like to have a father to look up to. His respond made me feel that I was missing out on so many things. I may be the Lord of Pinewood with all the wealth and lands but all of that seemed empty to me.

I woke up with the birds chirping their early morning songs. Peter was already awake preparing our breakfast. The sun was rising and not a dark cloud in the sky, and I think it was going to be another clear day ahead of us. I stood up and folded my blanket and placed it with the other belongings. I went to the river and washed my face with the cool fresh water and it felt good. I approached Peter to see if he needed help but everything was already prepared, our breakfast and coffee then I realized we were having fish.

"How did you catch this?" I asked in amazement.

Peter beamed, "With this my Lord," he showed me the long wooden stick with a pointy end which he was carving last night.

A chuckled, "A hunter and a spear fisherman." He laughed at the remark as well.

We harnessed our horses and packed our things after we ate. We rode off again with Peter leading the way. We were in Westwood on our way to the Steel Plants. It was a hot day so we had to take short breaks under a shade so not to tire the horses from the heat.

We finally arrived near the vicinity of the Steel Plants. There were about ten of them all surrounded by a very high wall. White smoke came from each Plant. There was nothing pleasant around this area, the Plants were an eyesore sticking out from the green lands of Pinewood. The horses were uneasy by the loud noises from the huge trucks that came and went through the large steel gate. The trucks loaded with tree trunks entered while the trucks with the steels sheets left. We finally reached the guard station who watched over the gate.

"Halt! No one is allowed to enter without a permit," shouted the guard.

We stopped in front of the gate and got down from our horses. The guard came to us holding a large firearm across his chest.

"This is Lord Curtis of house Bermule, we came to see Mr. Stanford," Peter informed the guard.

The guard in his silver uniform examined Peter then me and I don't think I was recognized, "Wait here," commanded the guard. He went back to the guard station and made a call. After a moment of talking, he returned and said, "Come with me."

We left the horses outside and the guard motioned the other guard to open the gates. The heavy steel slid open sideways and we entered. There were people going about inside the area and were wearing a worker's blue jumpsuit and silver helmets. The guard took us to a building which looked like an office. When we entered, a female receptionist behind a counter greeted us.

"They're here for Mr. Stanford," the guard reported.

"Thank you, I'll take it from here," the receptionist dismissed the guard.

She went out from the counter and approached us smiling and curtsied.

"Please follow me my Lord," she requested.

We followed her into an elevator and went up then stopped on the tenth floor. When we came out, we proceeded to a woman seated behind a table near a door.

"Lord Curtis here for Mr. Stanford," the receptionist informed.

The woman who seemed to be the assistant stood up

from her seat and curtsied, "Lord Curtis, this way please," she gestured to the door. The receptionist left us, and Peter stayed behind when I followed the assistant, she knocked and opened the door which revealed an office inside. A man was sitting behind a large wooden desk and behind him was a large window where you could see the Steel Plants outside. He looked up and stood from his chair and came towards me.

"Lord Curtis, please come in," he greeted.

The assistant introduced the man, "Lord Curtis, may I present to you Mr. Stanford, manager of the Bermule Steel Plants."

Mr. Stanford bowed and we shook hands. I couldn't tell how old he was but his brown hair and thick framed eyeglass and a few lines under eyes gave me the impression that he was a man of experience.

"Thank you Cora, that will be all," he dismissed his assistant. She nodded then exited the room.

"Please have a seat my Lord and what can I do for you?" he asked while he returned to his chair.

I took the seat in front of his desk and I responded casually, "I'm just here trying to familiarize the land, the Plants and the people. I recently returned from Fortis and I would like to be of some help here."

Mr. Stanford leaned on his large black leather chair and said, "The Duke of Pinewood is on top of things and he made it quite clear that everything should be where it is supposed to be my Lord so I assure you that everything is running smoothly, but if ever the time comes when we do need your advice, I won't hesitate to ask my Lord."

I nodded but I had a feeling that he was not sincere with his words.

"That's good to hear," I pretended to agree, "How's production?" I added.

"Better than ever my Lord, all Steel Plants are running at optimal level," he declared proudly.

"Any concerns from the workers?"

"None my Lord, everybody is contented with the wages and their job."

Mr. Stanford cleared his throat and shifted in his seat, "Anything else I could do for you my Lord?" he inquired.

I paused then finally asked, "You wouldn't mind if we could see inside one of the Plants?"

I could tell from his face that he was not happy with the idea, "I'm sorry my Lord, I could not allow you to enter for safety purposes of course; and besides, it's no place for a Lord, it's unpleasant and noisy. The Duke would not be happy if he found out about it."

It was not the unpleasantness of the place I was worried about; it was his deflection of the subject matter that bothered me. I was starting to get frustrated; I felt that no matter what I said, he would decline it directly or indirectly. It was obvious that he only takes orders from my brother and I can't persuade him any further if that was the case but I had to try.

"How about the living quarters then? Can I at least talk to some of the workers?" I implored to him.

He grinned uncomfortably and responded, "Everything is fine my Lord, I assure you....."

"Then you won't mind if I go there?" I insisted.

Mr. Stanford frowned and did not respond.

"Forgive me but I heard Mr. Stanford," I said calmly in a low voice yet trying to be intimidating, "that some were forced to work here."

Mr. Stanford chuckled, "All rumors. It would be unbecoming of you if you believed them..... my Lord."

"Is it?" I said, it was more of a provocation than a question.

He leaned forward his desk, with a calm and serious expression and I could not tell if he was affected by my words or not, "My Lord," he paused then proceeded, "we have been doing our job for a long time even when the late Duke, your father, was still around and I am very good at it. I assure you that nobody is forcing anybody to work here. It is against the law to force anyone to work against their will and you know that very well my Lord. The Duke of Pinewood does not allow any of the laws to be broken."

We sat in silence. I did not know what to think of this man but one thing was clear that he did not regard me as anything but a nuisance.

"If there's nothing else my Lord, please excuse me but I still have plenty of work to do," he stood up and I did the same and he guided me back to the door.

"Cora, please escort Lord Curtis, we're done here for today."

"Certainly sir," the assistant complied.

Mr. Stanford gave me one last look before I left, "Lord Curtis, it's been a pleasure having you here," he grinned like nothing had happened and he closed the door behind him without waiting for any reply.

We were on our horses again on a hilltop outside looking down at the white smokes being carried by the wind. I felt disappointed that I accomplished nothing, but there was not much I can do here then I sadly realized that the only man who probably knew everything was Andrew and he would not be happy if I questioned him. We went back to the road riding towards home. We were silent all the way as we galloped across the grass trying to reached home before dark and sometimes we had short breaks to rest the horses then we would be on our way again. We arrived home just in time it was almost dark. I thanked Peter and dismissed him before he returned the horses to Mr. Witherson. I entered the manor exhausted and was greeted by our butler Mr. Thistle.

"My Lord, dinner will be served at the dining room and his Grace and the Lady will be joining," he informed in a very formal manner.

"Thank you Mr. Thistle, let me have a change of clothes first," I said.

"Very good my Lord," he bowed then left.

I entered the dining room, it had a more intimate setting and a smaller table that accommodates ten people, and designed for the private dinners of the family. The room was not as big as our banquet halls but just as extravagant. Lady Katherine, Andrew's wife, was already seated waiting. She smiled when I approached and I smiled back. I took the seat across from her beside the head of the table. Lady Katherine was shy and a very refined attractive Lady, daughter of a very wealthy Duke. I saw her around the manor from time to time but we hardly spoke to each other not because I did not like her but she often kept to herself. She was known to be quiet in social gatherings and follows Andrew wherever he goes in such events and she does what he asked of her. Some might think of her as snobbish since she did not mingle like the others but I think of her as kind and friendly once she becomes comfortable with the company. She and my brother had two sons and a daughter. The sons were already at Fortis and soon their daughter, Katrina, will be sent away as well to Yuvaika. Lady Katherine usually spends her time in the west wing of the manor with her daughter who I met a few times, she had the same brown hair and light brown eyes as her mother, and nothing from Andrew. It was not long when Andrew entered the room, "Aaahh... good! I'm famished. Dinner Mr. Thistle!" he commanded while taking his seat at the head of the table. Mr. Thistle motioned the footmen to serve our food. No one spoke a word which was not unusual. We always waited for Andrew to speak first, and nobody wanted to dampened his mood, he had a temper and no one, not even Lady Katherine, would dare crossed him. We were already on our desserts when Andrew suddenly asked, "So how was your journey?" without looking up while he ate his cream pudding.

I was about to do the same but stopped midway, surprised by his question, "it was alright," I responded trying to make my answers as brief as possible.

"So you got a good look at the country side?"
"Yes I did."
"And the farms?"
"We visited a village along the way."
"Which village?"
"The one in Eastwood near Greendale forest."
"Ahhh... the First Village."
Then he paused.
"Where did you go next?" he continued.

I was not sure why he kept asking these questions but I had to answer him, "We went to the Steel Plants of Westwood."

Andrew stopped eating, drank his wine and wiped his mouth with a table napkin and finally looked at me for the first time that evening, "And do tell me what were you doing there?" he asked in a sudden change of tone of his voice, a more hostile manner.

I didn't answer immediately. Something told me that he already knew what I was doing there.

"Brother, I was only trying to familiarize how things work there," I explained defensively.

"By asking if I did something dishonorable?!" his voice was raised.

Mr. Stanford must have reported our conversation to him.

"I was not accusing anyone, I merely wanted to help if there were any concerns of the workers," I explained further.

Lady Katherine sat quietly in her seat, staring down the table as if trying not to get to my brother's attention.

Andrew angrily glared at me, "The concerns of the Steel Plants are none of your business but mine. How dare you question my work."

I did not answer, instead I continued to look down at my plate like a boy being scolded by his father.

"I expected more from you Curtis," he continued, "Don't forget that I am your Duke, I put the roof over your head, the clothes on your back, the food on your table, and everything you need. You should be careful, I could strip everything away from you," he angrily warned me, making it sound like I should be grateful for him.

Andrew then left fuming without saying another word and Lady Katherine followed not long after. I continued to sit there alone contemplating of what just happened. Foolish of me to ask questions, I should have kept my mouth shut. Sometimes trying to be good could get you into trouble and this was not the right time for that since I was trying my best to be Lord of Pinewood. I thought I was strong enough for this but I was wrong.

Three days had passed. I had spent most of my

time at the east wing trying to avoid Andrew. I was in the garden one sunny afternoon taking a stroll until a couple of birds distracted me with their singing while they played on the branches, I was amused as they hop around chasing each other. Miss Pattilyn did tell me that this was mother's favorite garden. It was a bit farther from the manor with grass hedges surrounding it and trees, and flowers of different colors. Birds would flock here and for some reason they prefer this garden. The two birds playing were at the fountain still chasing each other in the water. Beyond that, I saw Mr. Thistle coming my way. If he was here, Andrew must have sent him which made me suddenly uncomfortable.

"Lord Curtis," he called and bowed, "I'm glad I found you. His Grace would like to speak with you in his private office."

What does he want? Why can't he just leave me alone.

I followed Mr. Thistle back to the manor and we arrived at Andrew's office in the west wing.

"That would be all Mr. Thistle," Andrew dismissed him.

"Sit," he gestured me to take a seat on the coach while he poured wine in two glasses. He gave me the other glass and he sat at the couch across from me. He drank from his glass then placed it on the table in front of us. He looked at me with no trace of anger for the time being.

"Look Curtis," he began in a friendly approach, "I know you want to be useful, and I understand that, and I can't let my own brother be deprived of his duties. I know I need trustworthy men around, who better than my brother?" he paused and drank again from his glass.

"I can give you something to do, don't worry about it but not at the moment. First, I have something to make you feel more useful," he said grinning and excited about something that I was unaware of.

I was curious what he meant by that.

"So I decided to have you marry," he revealed with a huge grin on his face.

I was not expecting that. I knew I was going to marry but not this soon. Was this a joke? I had no idea what his intentions were but probably he plans to unite our House with another. I couldn't help but wonder though if this was out of kindness or pity, or for his own benefit.

"So? What do you think?" he asked enthusiastically.

I didn't know what to think. It was not like I had a choice and I knew I could not refuse him just because I was not ready.

"I guess..." I hesitantly and unwillingly obeyed.

"That's the spirit! I already sent the application so any day now we will find out who your mate will be."

"Wait, I thought you were going to choose who I marry?"

Andrew was puzzled then realized, "You mean bribe your match?" he laughed hard, "No no no," shaking his head, "It's more exciting this way isn't?" he declared with a coy smile.

It was then that I convinced that he was playing with me.

"Don't worry, I'm sure you'll be happy with your mate," he teasingly assured with no trace of ever being sincere as he raised his glass for a toast.

I was in my private chamber, spending my afternoon looking at the Pinewood maps. I would love to go out for another ride but it was drizzling. I needed time away from here especially after the conversation I had with Andrew a week ago. I barely slept after that. I did not know what to expect. Would I find happiness? Or an eternity of despair? Whatever happens I am stuck with whoever I was matched with, and there's nothing I can do about it.

Suddenly there was a soft knock at the door.

"Come in," I said without looking up from the map I was examining.

Peter entered and bowed.

"My Lord, you're being summoned by his Grace at the Parlour."

"Thank you Peter, I'll be right there."

Peter bowed again then left the room.

I arrived at the Parlour. Andrew was already there and a tall gentleman with pale blonde hair whom I saw around the manor was there as well. He had on a fine expensive business suit and wore a rimless glasses, and he never slouched, he also looked proud and very professional. They were sitting on the couch enjoying a cup of tea.

"Curtis, we've been waiting for you," Andrew said clearly in a good mood, "Please join us. I'm sure you've seen Mr. Logan around, he's my lawyer," referring to the gentleman beside him.

Mr. Logan tilted his head to a bow after being introduced. I took a seat across from them and Mr. Thistle served a cup of tea which I accepted.

"Leave us," Andrew commanded Mr. Thistle who obediently complied with a bow then left.

"What is this all about?" I asked unsure of what to expect.

Andrew beamed, "Mr. Logan here is a bearer of good news, show him," he ordered Mr. Logan who reached under his suit on his breast pocket and took out a gold envelope with black prints on it, then handed it to me. I reluctantly accepted and examined it. My name was written elegantly on the back in black ink, and I turned it over, there was the royal seal of half a moon and half a sun side by side in black and red wax. I glanced at Andrew and Mr. Logan then I carefully broke the seal and opened the envelope. Inside was a gold card with the letters written in black ink and I read the writings silently, then I could feel myself shaking in terror. I couldn't believe what I just read; I felt that my whole world had shattered. I was shaking my head and the word, "No" kept repeating on my lips. Andrew was confused and I knew he saw the obvious shock in my expression so he leaned over and snatched the card from my hand and silently read the letter for himself. He was frowning while reading but as he continued, his face lit up then he was grinning then he had difficulty finishing the letter because he was laughing so hard that he had tears in his eyes. He then passed the letter to Mr. Logan.

I did not find any of this funny. I was annoyed then I was furious at him.

"Fix this!" I commanded Andrew with a stern voice.

Andrew was running out of breath from laughing, he wiped the tears from his eyes and sighed heavily then shrugged his shoulders after he had calmed down and simply responded, "I can't."

"What?!" I raised my voice.

"I am not going to do anything illegal which you already accused me of and besides, fixing this would cost me a huge fortune," Andrew explained without any signs of remorse.

"I'll be the laughing stock of all the Elites," I angrily complained.

"So?" he said without any care while trying to suppress another laugh.

His words did not give me any comfort and it only made me madder.

"You did this, did you?" I blamed him and I could feel the blood rushing to my head.

Andrew became serious, "I did nothing of such sort but if you think that way then you have to accept your fate. I will not spend a single coin to make your life more convenient for you. I could care less."

Of all the people who had the power to undo this, it had to be Andrew, and the only thing that gave him the power was only because he was born first. My life was ending before I knew it. I never felt so helpless, overpowered, and defeated.

CHAPTER 4: THE PLEDGE

ELAINE

I woke up on a clear morning. I was getting ready for work welcoming another day where I expected that I would go down to eat breakfast and have an argument with mom, and a lovely talk with dad. Then I would be out of the house, see the man from across the street whom I had been trying to avoid ever since but to no avail. We only say hi and hello, and that was about it. I did not even bother to ask his name. I had no intention in putting a name to that handsome face; it was safer that way. After that, I would ride my bus to work. Do what I do at the clinic then make sure that Dr. Cook does not send me to another Elite client. Then at the end of the day, I would catch the bus back home, and glanced at the man from across the street again whose smile always gave me a weird feeling in my stomach. After that, dinner with mom and dad and talked about our day at work; and at night, I would lay in my bed while trying to stop myself from thinking about the man from across the street. This had been my routine but I was not complaining, I was more than satisfied living this way. I came downstairs for breakfast and as I entered the kitchen, I saw dad sitting on his chair but he was not reading his paper and mom was standing over the table, both were silent and staring at me. On the table, I saw a gold envelope with a black and red seal which I ignored and I did not know what was this all about but they were both acting strangely.

"Good morning honey, how was your sleep?" mom asked in a cheerful yet odd way.

Dad just sat there not speaking a word.

"It was fine," I reluctantly respond.

There was an unusual pause which made me very uncomfortable so I asked impatiently, "What's going on?"

"Oh honey! A letter arrived for you today," mom said cheerfully but I could hear a hint of nervousness. She took a brief glance at the table where the letter was.

"What's this?" I asked as I took the envelope from the table. I turned it around and my name was elegantly written on the back.

I was baffled what this was and where it came from but then it suddenly dawned on me. I dropped the envelope back to the table.

"No, I am not going to open it."

Mom gasped and scolded, "You would do no such thing Ellie, it is against the law to refuse a match."

"But I am not ready," I stubbornly insisted.

"No one is ever ready," mom exclaimed angrily.

Still I declined to open the letter. Mom was about to give me another lecture but dad interrupted, "Honey, Ellie," he addressed me with a calm and comforting voice, "I know this is difficult but we're here for you. We will always be there for you no matter what. You're strong Ellie, you can do this. We have faith in you."

Dad's words gave me the confidence I needed. I looked at him and mom, took the envelope, held my breath then opened it. I read carefully the card inside. Its content made my knees weak that I had to grab the nearest chair to sit before I would fall. My eyes were wide in shock, and my mouth opened.

"Is everything alright honey?" I heard my mom asked sounding extremely worried.

She took the card from me then read it, her expression turned from concern to being elated when she was done.

She gave the envelope to dad who became solemn after he read it.

"How... how is this possible?" I asked still in disbelief.

"We all knew that sometimes Betas could be matched with the Elites but it was extremely rare," mom replied while trying to hide her enthusiasm.

"But why me?"

Mom couldn't control it any longer, "Oh honey, don't you see? You will be a Lady, you will have your own manor, wealth and your own land. Everybody will respect you. You will have fine clothes and delicious food. You won't have to worry about paying the bills anymore."

She made it sound like it was a good thing.

"But I don't want to be a Lady. I don't want any of it," I cried, "I despise them, now I have to marry one of them?"

My tears came flowing freely on my cheeks. Everything was unfair. My life would never be the same again. Then I suddenly felt frightened, a Beta living among the Elites, I will be an outcast and never fitting in. I didn't even have a clue on how to be Lady.

Dad leaned towards me and took my hand while I was sobbing, he wiped my tears with his other hand and placed it gently on the side of my face, and he softly told me, "It's going to be alright Ellie, stop crying now. It is going to be hard, I know. We are not free to make the choices in our lives, our stations, our match but it is up to you what you make out of it, either you accept defeat and be miserable for the rest of your life, or make the best out of it, this is the only thing you can take control of," dad sighed and added, "You're going to be a Lady soon and what a fine and strong Lady you're going to be, and you're going to be different, but different is good. Your mother is right, you're going to be respected and revered and you're going to use that influence for something good. You can help more when you're an Elite Ellie, remember that."

We hugged and I held him tight like this might be the last time I get to hug him. Dad's words gave me solace and he was right, I should accept my fate and try to make the best of this. Mom started to cry and came over, and all three of us were hugging, and I felt so loved. We don't have much but we had each other and my heart was breaking knowing that I was going to leave them soon.

I left the house feeling down. The man from across the street smiled but became worried when I glanced at his direction then ignored him. I just walked aimlessly to the bus stop, trying my best to spend my day like nothing had happened. I lost focus at work and Dr. Cook took notice of it and asked if everything was okay.

"I'm fine," I replied unconvincingly.

Dr. Cook gave me a long look then declared, "You're clearly not fine Ellie, why don't you take some days off?"

"I'm fine Doctor," I insisted.

"You've been working hard Ellie, it's time to take a break and that is not a request."

I was tired and didn't want to argue. I left the clinic then went straight back home. I was looking out the window while riding the bus and I thought this might be my last few days here in Coastal City, and I am going to miss this place. I was surprised when mom was already home when I got back.

"Oh good Ellie, you're home. I left early from work today to buy you this," she excitedly said, nodding at the couch where there was a shopping bag on it.

"Go ahead, open it," she encouraged.

I opened the bag and inside was a black dress.

"A dress?" I asked curiously.

"Well that's for the Betrothal of course. You like it? Try it on," she urged.

That caught me off guard. I almost forgot about the Betrothal. It was when the match and their family would meet for the first time and agree on certain terms such as who gets to witness, where would the ceremony be, the living arrangements, and such.

"Maybe later mom, I'm sure it's nice," I was not in the mood.

I was about to go up to my room when mom called after me.

"Where are you going honey? Dinner will be served soon."

"I'll skip dinner tonight mom, I'm not hungry anyway," I went up to my room before she could say anything more. I lay on my bed until it got dark. It was getting late but I was still awake. I couldn't sleep because all the possible disaster that could happen when I marry kept running through my head. And a question kept on repeating, what was going to happen to me? I was distracted when I heard a soft tap on my window. It must be the wind. Then I heard another tap. I sat up and went towards the window, when I looked down, I saw under the moonlight the man from across the street standing in front, waving to get my attention. I was surprised to see him there. He gestured me to open the window.

"What are you doing here?" I asked in a low voice with a hint of urgency after I opened the window.

"Are you okay? Can we talk?" he asked sounding concern.

"Everything is fine," I lied, "and no we can't talk or it

will get us into trouble," I answered annoyed.

"I just want to talk, it won't take long I promise," he begged.

This was a very bad idea and could get us in trouble but the way he looked at me when he begged, I couldn't deny him.

"Alright, we'll talk by the entrance door but I am not letting you in. Just sit by the steps," I instructed.

He smiled and nodded in agreement and waited outside.

I looked at the time before I went down, it was pass one. What does he want to talk about at this time of hour?

I reached downstairs then silently unlocked the door and slowly opened a small crack, enough that we could hear each other clearly. I took a peek and he was there standing.

"I told you to turn your back at the door so that we won't seem suspicious," I scolded in a whisper.

"Oh!" he obliged, he turned then sat down by the door facing away from the house.

I sat on the floor and leaned against the wall beside the door hugging my knees.

"What do you want?" I murmured sounding uneasy.

"I just want to know if you're okay?" he gently whispered.

"I told you I'm fine."

"You didn't look fine this morning and when you came home," he said tenderly.

I sighed and firmly told him, "I said I'm fine so please leave, it's none of your concern anyway."

He paused then softly confessed, "You are always my concern Ellie."

I was startled by his remark. He cared for me but why? I leaned my head on the wall and faced the small opening of the door wishing that I could see his face. I did not say anything because I was afraid for us. What we were doing was against the law. As much as I want to tell him that I wish I could spend my life with him, I couldn't because it was impossible without putting ourselves in danger. I couldn't even say back to him that I cared for him too. I didn't want to give any hope to something that was already dead to begin with. This needs to end before it got out of hand.

"I received a letter today containing the name of my match," I sadly told him staring at the door as if I was talking to it.

He didn't answer right away. I wish I could see him so that I'll know what he was thinking.

"No one deserves you Ellie, you're too good for anyone, and if this was a free world, I would spend my entire life trying to prove myself to you," he softly proclaimed, "Life shouldn't be like this," he added sounding frustrated.

"But it is, so we must move on. Your turn will come, so we must forget each other," I affectionately begged him with finality and urgency.

"Yes my turn will come but I don't think I will ever forget you Ellie," he confessed passionately.

His words felt so good that it melted my heart but at the same time it hurts for I would never know what it would be like to freely reciprocate that kind of emotion.

"It's time to go."

"Wait! Don't you want to know my name?" he asked.

I wanted to tell him that I wanted to know his name more than anything.

"No I couldn't. It would be easier for me not to know..... if you truly care for me, you'd understand. I just want to remember you the way I remember you everyday..... as the man from across the street, goodbye," I painfully said my farewell then I stood up and shut the door without waiting for his reply. I stayed for a while thinking that this was the beginning of the end of my life.

The next morning, I woke up late and still tired. I wished everything yesterday was a dream and I was hoping that when I go down, everything would be the way it was. I lazily made my way downstairs without a care for anything and I was surprised when I found that both mom and dad were still at home.

"Mom, dad, why are you still here?"

"Well, your father and I took a leave from work for the Betrothal this afternoon," mom explained.

"Was it today?" I nervously asked.

"Yes, we received a message yesterday. The Betrothal will be at the Charmant Café three o'clock this afternoon."

"That's a very fine and expensive place," I anxiously observed.

"Yes, that's why I bought you that dress and you need to make yourself look presentable but don't worry I'll help you," she offered eagerly.

I groaned at the thought that I had to dress up today. I wished I could go just as myself; it was not like they can reject me if I didn't dress up at all.

We arrived at the café which was located at the northern part. It was an exquisite place full of elegantly designed mirrors and crystals. I couldn't help but look around admiring the splendidness and uniqueness of the place. We wore our finest clothes, dad was already uncomfortable with his suit just as I was with my dress but no matter how we tried to dress like them, we still stick out. The waiter led us to a private room which it seemed was rented for this event. When we entered, there was a tall man who looks like a few years older than me, with pale blonde hair and light complexion wearing a fine expensive suit and glasses. He stood up when he saw us approaching.

Was this man my match? There was nobody else in the room.

"Please have a seat," the man motioned us to take the seats across the long glass table from him. But before we pulled the chair, three waiters who were already standing behind did it for us. I was amazed by the fanciness of the place and I wondered if this was also the case where I would stay with my mate. The thought made my stomach churn and I suddenly felt nauseated.

More waiters came and served us tea and biscuit after we sat down.

The man also seated cleared his throat, "Shall we begin?" he asked in a very formal voice, "First let me introduce myself, I am Mr. Logan, the legal representative of His Grace, Lord Andrew Bermule, Duke of Pinewood."

"I'm Mr. Gertrue, this is my mate, and that's our daughter Elaine," dad awkwardly introduced us.

"Please to meet you all," he nodded but his expression remained blank.

"I..I.. thought we were meeting my daughter's mate and his family?" dad nervously stammered.

"His Grace and his brother Lord Curtis Bermule wished they could come, but they are preoccupied with other much more important matters, they convey their regrets and send me on their behalf instead," he explained still with no trace of any expression in his face.

Somehow I found it hard to believe what he just said.

"I understand," dad remarked.

"Let me read to you the conditions regarding the ceremony then," Mr. Logan continued while glancing at the paper then read it, "The ceremony will be ten days from now which will be held in Pinewood at the Bermule manor at exactly five o'clock in the afternoon. You will arrive on the day of the ceremony which of course you will be provided a private transportation from your house to Pinewood. Any questions before we continue?"

We sat in silence which then he assumed we had none.

"About the guest or the witnesses for the ceremony," he continued, "The Bermule family will make all the arrangements and the invitations."

"What do you mean? You mean we cannot invite our friends?" I blurted.

Mr. Logan turned to me and gave me an odd look as if I was out of place for interrupting but he replied anyway, "It is best that my Lords will take charge of the invitations for safety reasons."

"But...." I was about to object but dad placed his hand over mine and looked at me then shook his head, silently telling me not to argue which I obliged unhappily.

Mr. Logan glanced at me then at dad and continued reading, "Miss Elaine, after the ceremony, you will be known as Lady Elaine Bermule. You will reside at the Bermule manor with Lord Curtis and is expected to be at his side as your duty as a Lady." Mr. Logan stared at me once more waiting for me to react against it but I didn't because I was too appalled by the thought of it.

"When you become a Lady Miss Elaine, you are required to take a class on how to act and behave as a proper Lady by His Grace's orders. A teacher will be provided to you and the classes will be at the manor," Mr. Logan added.

They were trying to make me into one of those snobbish uptight Lady. Well, good luck to that. There was no way I was going to become one of them.

"And lastly," he looked up from his paper, "Miss Elaine after the ceremony, you'd be promoted to the stations of the Elite so normally you are expected not to be closely associated with any Betas or to share your private affairs to any of them."

"What?" disgusted by what he said. He was telling me that I would be too good to be around my friends and family when I become an Elite.

"And furthermore, you are not allowed to visit or communicate with your parents unless if His Grace allowed it."

We were horrified by Mr. Logan's last statement. It was bad enough that we could not see each other but to have permission, which may never be given, to see mom and dad was the last straw.

"Please, couldn't we visit her at least once a month?" mom pleaded.

"Or at least send messages?" I second her.

"Once a month is not that often and we promise it won't be any trouble," mom added almost crying.

Mom and I pleaded together hoping that he would reconsider.

Mr. Logan was calm and unaffected by our request, it was like talking to a cold statue. Then dad spoke, "Please, could we at least have this? Allow us to visit her, it does not have to be often."

"Mr. Gertrue, let me remind you that Miss Elaine will be an Elite and by marriage to Lord Curtis her loyalty is bound only to the Duke of Pinewood which should be absolute."

We were speechless. If becoming an Elite meant following more rules, then I didn't want to be a part of it.

"And because Miss Elaine will be an Elite after the ceremony, your presence Mr. and Mrs. Gertrue at the banquet is no longer required," he said further without any remorse.

It was hopeless, these Elites and their protocols only meant they didn't want anyone below their station to be among them. I knew Mr. Logan were only following orders but still it didn't stop me from feeling angry towards him, he was a rich Alpha and not any different from them, and the way he handled himself, being aloof and proud only infuriates me more.

We left the café after everything was settled and rode the bus home. None of us wanted to talk about what happened that day when we arrived at the house.

"I can't do this dad," I broke sobbing on his shoulder when he came over to hug me.

Mom was fighting off tears herself.

"Remember Ellie," he looked at me and touched my chin, "You are strong. There's nobody else I could think of who is strong enough to do this."

"It's okay honey," mom reassured me while she touched my shoulder.

"What if it will never be okay? What if…. I ran away?" It was an idea out of desperation.

Mom and dad looked at each other.

"Then you'll be running forever Ellie," mom spoke.

"Yes but it will be a fate better than what waits for me," I explained with optimism.

Dad was sadly shaking his head, "That's not a good idea Ellie, the Protectors will not stop searching for you and they will not stop coming for me and your mom."

"There is no way out of this is there?" I asked hopelessly.

Dad shook his head without saying a word only meant he cannot help me with this. I had no choice but to accept my fate. There was no way around this without endangering the lives of my family and the people I knew. I had to face the worst to come and there was no room for weakness.

The morning on the day of the ceremony was finally upon us. We made our final preparations for the last couple of days. I resigned from work, I told the staff that I was matched and had to relocate somewhere far from here. We were all sad and in tears when we finally said our goodbyes. It was harder saying farewell to Dr. Cook and Sarah whom I would miss more and probably never see again. I was seated on a chair inside my room in front of the mirror while mom fixed my hair and applied make up on my face. She let my long wavy auburn hair loose and it dangled below my shoulders. Then she placed a silver brooch shape like a flower. I wore a green Lady's banquet gown that showed my bare shoulders and it had little white stones that glittered on the green embroidery on the long sleeves and chest, with a tight corset underneath and a long wide skirt almost touching the floor; we picked this together yesterday in one of those expensive Elite shops. The price was far beyond our means but mom insisted I wear the most beautiful gown in my ceremony. I didn't see the point though on spending our money on this expensive gown that I probably was going to wear only once but I was grateful to her, she was indeed a caring mother and despite how many times we argued, I was going to miss her terribly.

"Thank you mom," I said sincerely, then she stopped what she was doing looking bewildered, "Thank you for everything, for your love and care, I couldn't ask for anything more," I continued while I could feel myself tearing up.

"Oh honey," she happily reacted and gently hug me from behind careful not to crumple my hair or the gown. I touched her arm that she wrapped around me, and we smiled then giggled.

"I love you and I am going to miss you everyday Ellie," she expressed with tender affection and gently kissed me on the cheek.

    I went downstairs careful not to trip. Dad was waiting for us in the living room wearing his black formal suit and mom followed me down wearing her light blue dress that she only wore during special occasions. Dad looked at me in awe and said, "You look beautiful."

I smiled then went to him and straightened his suit, "You're not bad yourself dad," I complimented. Then he glanced at mom gleaming, "You look stunning my dear, just like the first time I met you." Mom smiled then gave dad a small kiss on the lips.

"Are we ready? The car is waiting outside," dad asked.

"We're ready," mom declared.

Mom and dad went out the house first. I stayed behind for a bit looking around one last time. I will miss this place, all the happy and sad memories. I will miss my room most especially, where I found my solace whenever I was down and the only place I was free with my thoughts but that was over, it was time to let go. I said my silent goodbye to the place but it was more of saying goodbye to my childhood and the familiar. I followed mom and dad outside where they patiently waited beside an expensive looking car. I was not allowed to bring anything with me; Mr. Logan informed us that everything that I needed would be provided as soon as I arrive at the manor. The driver in his silver uniform was waiting outside the car door, and he immediately open the back passenger side when we approached. It was our first time to ride such a luxurious vehicle. The neighbors noticed the car which clearly stood out around this neighborhood then small crowd started to gather to watch, and whisper among themselves before the car slowly started to leave. Gossip of a Beta who was matched with an Elite started to circulate among the neighbors since a couple of days ago and I was sure that would be what they would be talking about for days to come until they grew tired of it. I didn't notice the man from across the street. I was avoiding him since that night he came over but I knew he was there but there was no looking back as we drove farther away.

    We stopped at a shuttle dock in the city where a shuttle was waiting to take us to Pinewood. We were greeted by two smiling women who I thought were the servers when we boarded. It was a large silver shuttle, bigger than our house or any other house in the neighborhood. I started to feel anxious when we took off because I hated flying but it disappeared when I couldn't even tell if we were ascending or if we were flying unlike the public shuttle we rode before where the ride was noisy and rough. There was a silver table which was full of treats and drinks laid out by the servers. They asked us if we needed anything from the table. I told her that I would like to take a look first since I was not used to being served. Everything in the table looked amazing and delicious that I didn't know what to choose. The female server must have noticed then she respectfully told me that I can pick anything or even everything I want since it was just all for us. I was amazed by the display on the table that I wanted to try everything but my nerves for the ceremony got the best of me that I lost my appetite. We were silent for the rest of the trip, our nervousness was to blame but I entertained myself to take my mind off what was to come by looking out the window admiring the clouds of different shapes and sizes but when the server announced that we will be flying over Pinewood, I started to feel incredibly uneasy. This was it, I never felt so nervous before. I would be meeting my mate, his family and every Elite acquainted to them. It was going to be my first time to see so many proud and vain Elites. What was I going to say to them? The only Elite I have talked to was Lady Georgina and she was terrible. I saw some of the Elites when I was at the Yuvaika Institute before and they were the type of girls who I would never want to be friends with. I was sure that my mate would be the same. My palms suddenly started to sweat, how long was this going to be?

    I looked down the window and saw nothing but green. Trees and grasses were everywhere. The sight of horses running freely across the grass as the shuttle passed made my heart skipped a beat. I have never seen so many of them in one place before. Although the sun was shining and was made to be a lovely day but nothing could cheer me up. Maybe if this was any other ordinary day I would be excited to have visited a beautiful new place such as Pinewood but not this time, I wanted to leave this place instead. The female server announced that we would be docking soon. The shuttle began to descend then finally landed. There was another car waiting for us when we went down from the shuttle and we rode without knowing where it would take us. We passed some more trees and flocks of birds flew over, this land was obviously a sanctuary for many wildlife I thought. After a few minutes, we arrived at a large tall gate made out of black steel bars with artistic design. It automatically opened as we stopped in front and closed after we went through. Tall trimmed trees were aligned on each side of the road and it went on and on like they were guarding the path. We finally slowed down near a garden and at the center of it was a large white structure with no walls and was made out of white marble. It was supported by large pillars with a hint of silver designs like roots crawling on them but gracefully. In between the pillars were white thin see through fabric that dangled from the top all the way almost touching the floor and covered the entire sides of the structure and it dances when blown by the wind. The car stopped a few meters away. I was starting to breath heavily; I could see that there were people already inside. Dad noticed that I was terrified so he took my hand and gave it a soft squeeze. A man in fine silver coat approached and opened the car door for us. My heart was pounding and it felt like it was going to leap out from my chest.

"Please, this way," the man holding the car door instructed us and gestured his hand showing us the way.

We went out the car reluctantly and followed the man who led us to the white structure but asked us to wait first just outside.

"Before we go in, the parents should enter after the Lady but would not join her at the Pledge table. You are to turn to the left side when you reached the front. The Lady then proceed until she is beside the Lord and wait for the judge to begin the ceremony," the man explained to us with preciseness.

He paused for a while and glanced at us one by one trying to see if we heard him and understood.

"After the ceremony, the parents may say their goodbyes before leaving. A car will be waiting to take you to the shuttle docks which will take you back where you came from," he continued.

I looked at mom and dad who were as nervous as I was, I felt like crying at the thought that they were leaving for good after this.

"Shall we proceed?" the man asked.

"No wait! Could you give us a minute?" I requested desperately.

The man was startled but nodded giving me consent.

I walked not far away but was still in eyesight of him, and then mom and dad followed me not far behind. I was pacing back and forth, and breathing heavily.

"Are you okay honey?" mom asked sounding worried.

"Just terrified," I responded while still pacing.

"Ellie," dad stopped me then placed his hands on my shoulders and looked at me straight in the eyes and said, "you're better than them, remember that."

I looked back directly at him, his eyes told me that I could do this and I just had to believe then I took one deep breath and let it out.

"Okay, I'm ready."

We went back to the man who was waiting for us. I could see that more people were arriving in their very fine and expensive gowns and suits. The man held the thin white fabric at the entrance motioning us to enter. I came inside first as instructed and I was holding my breath and mom and dad followed. The structure from the inside had a high white ceiling carved with elegant designs and breathtaking crystal chandeliers designed with elegant silver like tree branches were dangling from the ceiling illuminating more brightly than white stars and when you looked around, no tables or chairs could be seen. Everybody was extravagant that I felt underdressed for the occasion. The people inside were standing and talking amongst themselves but when some of them noticed that I was entering, they fell silent, so silent that it was eerie. They made way for me to pass while continuing to stare, I couldn't make out what they were thinking but some gave a cold and piercing stare, and some of disgust that made me so uncomfortable that I wanted to hide or run away. But I tried not to look down, determined to show that I was unmoved by all of these and that they cannot break me. They were not the only ones who knew how to be indifferent. I walked slowly to the front where the judge was waiting. Were all ceremonies like this? Silent and cold? I recalled Sarah shared to me once about what her own ceremony was like and she said hers was simple and brief, and it was not a celebration. Was this worse than hers? I was halfway and they continued to stare, and not a familiar face in sight. This would have been easier if some of my friends were here. I reached at the Pledge area and I saw at my right side, a Lord with sandy brown hair and dark brown eyes sneering at me. Mom and dad took their place to the left. As I approached the Pledge table, I saw a tall man standing in front of the judge with his back towards me, he had a long black hair and wore a silver tailcoat made from the finest fiber with a white soft undershirt under a smooth dark blue collared vest, silver pants tucked in his long black boots. Everybody was looking at me except for him. He was facing the judge all the time, but when he finally turned his head to glance at me as I stood beside him, I saw that he was one of the most gorgeous man I have ever seen but his piercing blue eyes were cold and distant, deprived of any signs of emotion and he seemed unhappy as I was. I was not hoping for anything before I met him but I couldn't help being disappointed that he was just like any other Elites present there, heartless, and his presence screamed every bit of it. I stood in front at the Pledge table beside him facing the judge who was unwelcoming as the rest of them. He began the ceremony with the introduction on the purpose of why we were gathered and read parts of the law that required us to be together and reminded us of the consequences if we broke this pledge. He kept on reading about the laws and there were so many of them but I didn't hear him because I was preoccupied with my own thoughts.

"Miss Gertrue, how do you respond?" he suddenly asked.

I was puzzled staring at the judge then I realize he was referring to me and then I started to panic. What was the question? Was there something that I was supposed to say?

The judge cleared his throat uncomfortably and repeated slowly, "With the words I have read, will you abide by the laws of the Empire with all your power and without doubt, and accept your match as chosen by the Numen for you?"

So I was supposed to respond to this? It was silly that

they needed to ask such questions when there was only one answer allowed.

"I will," I responded.

I could hear a low sniffle from behind me and I could tell that it could only be mom.

The judge nodded at my answer then turned to the man beside me, "Lord Curtis, with the words I read, will you abide by the laws of the Empire with all your power and without doubt, and accept your match as chosen by the Numen for you?"

"I will," he said in a serious voice.

The judge declared that our bond was legal and to validate it, he showed us a contract which was too long to read then he requested us to sign our names on one of the blanks below the document. We both obliged then the judge signed his own name after and affixed his seal with red wax at the bottom then rolled the paper and kept it.

"Before the ceremony ends, it is time for Miss Gertrue's ascension to the Elite station," the judge proclaimed looking at my direction. He explained briefly the responsibilities of being a Lady and others until he finally said, "Do you swear upon your life to pledge allegiance to the Duke of Pinewood and to the House of Bermule and give your unconditional loyalty?"

It was bad enough that I had to marry one of them but I had to declare my undying fidelity to a person who I did not know or to the family I knew nothing about, and I doubt they would do the same for me. But again, there was only one answer allowed, "I do," I responded deprived of all truth in it.

The judge then took another contract and had me sign, "Please sign your new name Lady Elaine Bermule." I hesitated, the name sounds unnatural to me. I didn't want it, my name was all I had and even that they were taking it away from me but I told myself that it was only a name, you may have a new name but it doesn't change who you are. So I unwillingly signed the paper.

"Now my Lords and Ladies, may I present to you Lady Elaine Bermule of Pinewood," the judge formally announced.

There were a few soft claps, they seemed unsure if they were even allowed to then eventually died down.

"The ceremony has ended," the judge declared to the crowd behind us then he faced me, "You may say your goodbyes," he told me specifically in a low voice. I went to where mom and dad stood, disregarding everyone else's glances. Tears started to form in our eyes. I hugged them both as tight as I could and whispered I love you.

"Take care of yourself Ellie," mom said sobbing.

"You'll always be my little Ellie, no matter what," dad lovingly said wiping a tear away from my cheek.

The man who brought us here suddenly appeared, "It is time Mr. and Mrs. Gertrue."

I wiped away my tears and held their hand one last time, not wanting to let go as they started to walk away.

"Goodbye," I told them.

They looked at me one last time and whispered goodbye as well then left with dad's arm around mom as he comforted her when she sobbed some more.

  I felt lonely being there. A stranger who did not belonged. They all seem to know each other but neither one of them had a friendly face. None of them would ever feel the way I felt that night. I was different, and for the Elites, that meant I was unworthy. I stood alone while everyone else took their time to talk to one another. It was amusing to watch them though, they converse with such grace and were very reserved, probably trying to be agreeable. Still each of them had different personalities and those who lavished the attention were the most pretentious of them all. Curtis was having what seemed to be a serious conversation with a blond hair and gray eyed man and the way he stood and his appearance, which was better than others, could no doubt be another very wealthy Lord. They looked unhappy though while conversing and Curtis face was gloomy as ever. The Lord that sneered earlier when I passed came over where I stood.

"Lady Elaine Bermule, how does it sound?" he asked grinning and I didn't like the sound of his tone. I could tell that this man was distinctly obnoxious and provocative.

I didn't answer right away, instead, I gave him a hard look, gauging him and showing no signs of fear.

"No complains here yet," I responded coldly and sounding bored yet annoyed.

"Hahaha," he laughed, "You're a headstrong woman aren't you?"

"Only when provoked," I responded irritated.

"Well let me tell you something," he sounded suddenly serious and grim, "You may have an Elite name and a title but never forget that you were nothing before all this," he coldly stared like I was the lowest form of creature in this room. Then like a switch, he changed his mood, he smiled at me as if he was only kidding and said, "Anyway, welcome to Pinewood my Lady, I hope you don't get lost in the woods." I had no idea if he said it out of concern or out of spite but I didn't bother responding to him and I grew tired playing his games. Then I realized that Curtis and the Lord beside him stopped talking and was staring at my direction. The man who accompanied mom and dad returned then bowed at the Lord who was talking to me and said politely, "Your Grace, may I?" It dawned on me that I was talking to the Duke of Pinewood, and then I felt my blood drained from my face. He could have thrown me in prison if he wanted to for the disrespectful way I treated him. I should have stayed quiet and minded my own business.

"Yes make the announcement Mr. Thistle," Andrew consented sounding annoyed.

Mr. Thistle cleared his throat, "My Lords and Ladies, if you would be so kind to proceed to the manor, the banquet is about to begin. Thank you."

Everyone started to leave and rode their cars going to the manor. The Duke who was still standing beside me smiled mockingly, "You're riding with your new mate, my Lady," he made a quick glance at Curtis who was nearby and could have overheard him then smirked and left. Curtis didn't bother to talk. He glanced at my direction then walked passed me without saying a word. I didn't know what else to do so I followed him. I was outside when I saw him ride the car that was meant for us, and I hesitantly got inside after him. The driver closed the door then we sat in awkward silence. I was at the other end of the seat while Curtis was on the other, staring out the window ignoring me. Then the car drove off. I didn't mind the silence; it was welcomed for once since I didn't want to speak to him too. But the only reason he was not speaking to me was because I did not deserved his attention or even his time which made me resent him more. We passed by magnificent gardens before we reached the manor. It was one of the largest houses I have seen, I found it hard to believe that that's a house with the size and extravagance of it all. Its excessiveness and brilliance I was in awe but it disgusted me at the same time. Back home, Omegas had a hard time, and yet the Elites on the other hand, spend their wealth on things they do not need, and the sad part was that I was amongst them. Our car stopped at the driveway in front of the manor. A footman opened the car door and Curtis exited first then I followed. Lords and Ladies were pouring through the double door entrance and into a very large hall. Mr. Thistle saw us arriving then he walked towards us.

"Lord Curtis, it is customary for the Lord to offer his arm to his Lady in a social occasion such as this," he reminded respectfully almost in a whisper then bowed subtly and left. Curtis didn't say anything but it was clear that he was uncomfortable but he offered his arm to me nevertheless. Play the game and pretend to go with it, I told myself even though I was uneasy with this too. I unwillingly slipped my hand under his arm and we were walking side by side like the rest of the Elites there. He led me to a large banquet hall with layers and layers of extravagant glass chandeliers with yellow lights and gigantic pillars surrounded the hall that was as white as the marble floors and large windows covered the walls draped with majestic royal blue and silver curtains. When we entered, I noticed that there were more guest here than at the ceremony. I suddenly felt very nervous, I held Curtis' arm tight even though I didn't prefer it and I ignored his reaction to my sudden change in grip. A footman announced our arrival and as he did, everyone in the hall was now watching us in silence except for the orchestra playing at the middle of the banquet. We went down the wide stairs with dark royal blue carpet that stretched on it and it seemed like it took forever before we reached the bottom.

Don't fall, don't fall, I kept telling myself.

I sensed that all eyes were on me, staring through maybe hoping to get a piece of who I was. I was a display to them, there to be judged freely. I wanted to bury myself. We finally reached the end of the stairs and slowly made our way through a corner with less people, and to my relief, everybody stopped staring by then. We were near a large pillar when I finally let go of Curtis' arm and I immediately hid behind it leaving Curtis where he was then I released my breath that I didn't notice I was holding all this time. I leaned myself on the pillar and slouched on it, my feet were hurting from the heels I wore and my gown suddenly became tight making it hard to breathe. I wanted to cry but I didn't want to be defeated or they would have thought of me as weak. Eventually, I composed myself and straightened my gown and fixed my hair then I emerged from behind the pillar and rejoined Curtis. He was joined by the Lord he was talking to at the ceremony. The Lord was grinning when he saw me approaching, and his friendly and welcoming smile took me by surprise then I stood not too close beside Curtis. I didn't react to the Lord's friendliness because I was not sure if he was sincere or not, or if he was there to mock me like the rest of the Elites.

"Well Curtis aren't you going to introduce me to the lovely Lady?" he spoke cheerfully.

I saw on Curtis' expression that he was annoyed by what he said but obliged though, "Ambrose this is Lady Elaine."

Ambrose was beaming gave a small bow and happily said, "It's my pleasure to meet you my Lady. Curtis and I are very good friends and I hoped we could be too."

"It's nice to meet you too my Lord," I greeted respectfully still hesitant of his intentions.

A footman holding a round silver tray served us glasses with wine. Ambrose took two and gave one to me which I accepted. Curtis took a glass for himself then we drank our wine. It was my first time tasting such expensive wine and I admit that it was beyond what I expected, and I liked the way it soothed my nerves.

"How's the wine my Lady," Ambrose asked.

"Very nice my Lord," I answered shyly.

He smiled and came closer as if he was about to share a secret.

"Don't worry, they'll soon get bored of you and leave you alone, and you'll get use to them around," he assured me in a comforting tone. That was the only nice thing that anybody had said to me the entire night. He must had notice I was tense and it was then that I realized that Ambrose was not like any of the Elites, although he stood tall and wore fine clothes, he had an aura in him that made him seem approachable and reliable. He was handsome as well, in a different way from Curtis and he was easier to be with. I glanced at Curtis trying to get his reaction but he remained standing looking nowhere in particular unmoved by everything. Ambrose must have noticed that he blurted, "Oh, and you'll get use to Curtis as well, don't worry," he chuckled. Curtis seem confused then annoyed by his words and I didn't share Ambrose's humor regarding this but I was grateful that he was trying to lighten the mood. Then Food came in small bite sizes on a tray that the footmen served. The three of us continued to stay away from the crowded parts and Ambrose took the liberty of talking out of earshot from the rest about some of the Elites who were there. He was telling me where they were from and their personalities and their background, and sometimes he would make funny comments about them. He made me feel relaxed and I knew he only did this to help me feel more comfortable but I was still careful around him, making sure I didn't speak or show signs of what I thought about what he said. I stood there carefully listening to him and smiled only when needed while he continued to talk about the Elites around us. Curtis didn't joined the conversation though as he continued to be aloof.

"…. And that's Lord Featherhorne of Novature. His lands are rich in salt," Ambrose spoke in a low voice that I could hear as he discreetly pointed at a short plump Lord with an odd hair and wearing a tight and colorful ensemble, "He is very rich and guess where he spends his wealth on?" Ambrose asked excitedly.

"I honestly don't have a clue," I smiled while starting to enjoy his game.

"Buttons!" he chuckled as he revealed.

I tried not to laugh at his answer but I thought it was very funny though.

"Silly is it? I heard he has thousands of buttons in a room in all shapes and sizes, and no one knows why he collects them but I think he just wants to put buttons everywhere. Please don't tell anyone I told you that," he pleaded while grinning at his own jest. For a brief moment I was enjoying Ambrose's company and forgot where I was, I always thought Elites to be silly in their fancy clothes and excessiveness but I had no idea they could be odd and funny at the same time. It all changed though when Curtis suddenly spoke angrily in a low voice, "What is he doing here?"

Ambrose and I were startled by his sudden reaction. I could see Curtis' expression change to a look full of hatred and disgust. I realized that he was glaring at someone who was approaching in our direction. A Lord wearing a mocking smile was slowly making his way to us and Ambrose's mood changed as well when he saw him. We remained silent until the Lord arrived to where we were, laughing and clapping in a teasing way.

"Well Curtis you have outdone yourself this time, the first to get married and with a Beta!" he teased shaking his head in a mocking way.

"Leave us alone Stephen," Ambrose threatened him.

"Relax Ambrose, I just came to congratulate Curtis and his new Lady," he spoke sarcastically.

He was grinning at Curtis, "Congratulations for making a fool of yourself. I heard that your brother didn't even bother paying to change the match. I guess he wanted some fun but I don't blame him, it was starting to get dull around here," he laughed at his own ridicule.

"Be careful with your words Stephen or I'll...." Curtis angrily warned him. I could see that he was furious and almost lost his temper until Ambrose hurriedly stepped in between them.

"He's not worth it Curtis," Ambrose spoke trying to calm him down.

Stephen continued to laugh and was looking at my direction like a predator stalking its prey. He circled me and was examining from head to toe and I suddenly started feeling afraid by his intimidating presence. He became serious while staring directly at me face to face, "But I have to hand it you Curtis, you have a very beautiful specimen here. Who would have thought they have such beauty in the lower stations. Too bad you could have been mine if you were an Elite," he insinuated with such inappropriate desire by the sound of his voice.

"Enough Stephen," Ambrose commanded forcefully this time.

Stephen conceded unwillingly. The way he talked made me feel that I was not a person but a piece of property, someone to be used for the envy of others. He was the worse of them lot. He stood beside me and whispered something in my ear, "You see that Lord and the Lady not far from him?" he spoke in a hushed and disturbing way referring to the middle aged Lord who was talking loudly in front of us at a distance, and a tall Lady who was having a conversation with the other Ladies but looked bored.

"They've been married for more than thirty years," he said while briefly glancing at Curtis, "yet they have never slept together in the same room since they got married, never ate at the same table except on social occasions, and never talked to each other when at home. If they do talk, it only ends up one insulting the other. Your life is going to end up like that, with no sense of direction or a future. What a waste would that be for someone as pretty as you," he sounded contented with his threats.

Tears were starting to form and it was getting harder to breath but I told myself not to cry trying to keep the tears from falling. I stared back at Stephen hoping that he would see that his words didn't affect me and at the same time trying to keep myself together not to break down in front of him.

"It was nice meeting you my Lord. I am sure you have far more better ways to spend your time than talking to a low birth like me who obviously does not deserve your presence. Good evening," I politely spoke hoping that he didn't notice my difficulty saying those words. I curtsied wishing he understood that I wanted him to leave. It was the first time I spoke to him that night and it made Stephen laughed then he slowly bowed, I was relieved he took the hint, and then he finally left us without saying another word. Curtis and Ambrose still wore their angry faces. Anguish overcame me and I suddenly felt exhausted that my strength started to faltered.

"I apologized for Stephen. His manner was inexcusable; I hope you won't pay much attention to him," Ambrose spoke and had a look of concern.

Curtis remained silent showing no signs of remorse. Does he loathe me as much as Stephen or the other Elites? But what could I expect from him? He was the same as the rest of them; they have no regard for stations beneath them, and even though I was Elite through marriage they would never see me as their equals. I realized that I would never be capable of loving Curtis and he was incapable of such affections as well. The night was late and the guest finally started to leave, and I saw Andrew walking towards us.

"Say your goodbyes now Lord Ambrose," Andrew commanded looking bored.

Ambrose could not refuse the Duke so he nodded and briefly whispered something in Curtis' ear then patted his shoulder before he solemnly took his leave. Andrew waited until he left then he tiredly smiled at us and said, "Well, it's time to do your duty my brother. Sharing the bed with your mate is customary on the first night after the ceremony," he spoke with a sheepish grin then added, "Seal the bond," it sounded more like a command when he left us in our awkwardness.

I was terrified when we left the banquet hall. We made our way through the large hallway as I silently followed Curtis. Seal the bond, it was not required by law but was it expected with the Elites on their first night? The white hallway was elegant and the walls were designed with artistic carvings that only skillful hands could do, and the wall lamps were lit and they looked like dancing fires burning brightly along the hallway. The night was beautiful and peaceful but when you are with a stranger then this was not a night of sweet dreams, no passionate lovers, no affection or devotion; these simply did not exist in my own story. We stopped at a large door where a footman who was standing guard opened it. We entered in which I assumed was our bed chamber, then the door closed after. The room was dimly lit, and was ten times larger than my own bedroom back home. It had a large balcony with glass doors overlooking the gardens outside. The chamber had its own living room with a couch and a table, and a soft blue carpet laid on the marble floor. The windows were draped with sophisticated blue curtains, and the large bed with white sheets and pillows, and the blanket covered by blue linen was on the center against the wall with classic mounted lamps placed on each side of the bed. Curtis went inside a room within the chamber, and I went to explore the other room opposite to where he was, and when I entered, it was not as small as I thought it would be, it was brighter inside with white lights illuminating the entire ceiling and walls and even the floor. It was full of expensive female wardrobes that only a Lady Elite would wear, long fine dresses with wide skirts for daily use either long sleeved or without, some showed bare shoulder and the chest while some covered the neck, and banquet gowns with elegant and extravagant designs all hanged neatly and organized according to color. There were boots, shoes, heels and sandals also organized by color and type and displayed like they do on the shops. Hand bags of the most expensive kind where placed inside glass cases according to colors and types, and I was amazed when I saw a bag glittered with what I thought were real diamonds, and large clear mirrors were placed on each side of the walls. I wearily looked around and thought I only needed something comfortable to wear for sleeping. I found a white silk short nightgown, I never wore this kind of clothes when I sleep but it was all that was there. I covered myself with a white soft robe uncomfortable that I had to wear something revealing.

Then I heard a soft knock outside the main door.

"Yes?" I overheard Curtis say and it seemed that he was already in the bedroom.

Then the door slowly creaked and I heard a woman spoke kindly, "Pardon me my Lord for intruding but I was wondering if the Lady needed any assistance?"

"You may come in Miss Pattilyn," Curtis gave permission.

Then I heard footsteps approaching the room where I was and then she appeared with a pleasant smile.

"My Lady," she curtsied, "May I congratulate you on your marriage. I am here to convey my assistance my Lady, if you need any," she offered pleasantly.

I couldn't help but smile back, "Thank you but none at the moment."

"Well then... Oh!" she saw my gown lying on the floor, "I can take that for you my Lady." She picks up the gown and slings it over her arm.

"Can I keep it?" I quickly pleaded, "My mom bought it for me." It was the only thing I had from back home I thought.

"Certainly my Lady, let me just have someone wash it for you and I'll return it when it is done."

"Thank you," I spoke feeling grateful.

"Is there anything else my Lady?"

"No, that would be all." But in the back of my mind I was thinking if she could take me far away from here.

"I'll take my leave then, good night my Lady," she curtsied then I followed her to the bedroom.

"Good night my Lord," she curtsied and then left us.

We were alone again. Curtis was on the couch and I was on my side of the chamber. For once, he looked at me but I couldn't make out what he was thinking in the dim room and it made me so uneasy that I quickly tightly closed the robe I was wearing. There was no sound except for my heavy breathing. Was this really happening? I prayed that it wouldn't, not with him. It took all of my strength whatever was left to stop myself from trembling. He was my mate and a Lord so he can do whatever he wanted should he decide to take me tonight. He overpowered me, and what I wanted had nothing to do here and it didn't matter. He suddenly moved then stood up which startled me. I thought he was coming towards where I was but he went to the bed instead, and took a pillow, and for the first time that night he spoke to me with a somber manner, "You can take the bed," and he went back to the couch and placed the pillow then lay down. I was so relieved and it felt like something heavy was lifted from me. I was grateful that he decided not to do anything tonight. I went to the bed and settled under the comfortable blanket while still wearing my robe. I turned off the lamps with the switch on my side of the bed. I was still awake thinking of what had just happened. I miss mom and dad, I miss our home, and I even miss the man from across the street. I wondered what he was doing, was he thinking of me? Then I didn't realize that I was crying, I was holding back tears the entire night that it all finally came streaming down my face. I was tired of being strong that it was time to let the tears go, and I didn't even care if Curtis heard. There was clearly no connection between us, not like what mom and dad had. He despises me as much as I do him. Although this was a foolish thought, but I blamed him for everything because if it wasn't for him, if only he didn't existed then I wouldn't be here in this miserable place away from home. Suddenly I felt exhausted; the day had worn me out. I finally closed my eyes. My only desire was to sleep and dream of nothing but home and those dreams would be the closest thing I had left of the place.

CHAPTER 5: LOST SOULS

CURTIS

I knew my matched with a Beta was the worst thing that could happen to me; being the topic of gossip, their fake smiles, and the whispers behind my back. I was disgraced when my own brother didn't fix the match when he could. I was furious at Andrew, I still believed he did this on purpose just his way of making my life miserable for disappointing him or even father. I wanted revenge but it would be treason which was punishable by death so that was pointless.

It had been a month since the ceremony and nothing was getting any better. Even before the ceremony, things began to stir among the Elites and among the household staff that a Lord was matched with a Beta. The news was like a disease with the Elites that they thought it was contagious as they looked at me with revolting expression. They thought I wouldn't notice but their inconspicuous behavior made it hard to miss. The arrival of Elaine was most anticipated and Andrew was having fun with the unconventional event. Everybody was curious who she was but I was probably the only one who was not. They saw her as some kind of bizarre new species that they can't wait to be entertained. I must admit though, she was very alluring at the ceremony, like a rare creature, different in a captivating way but still she only reminded me of how Andrew was turning my life upside down. I was silently begging for her to not go through with the Pledge, sparing me from this doomed life. Ambrose as usual, always found kind words to say, such as, it could have been worst at least she was not bad looking, or, maybe you'll learn to love her, but I was not paying much attention to him. I commend her for her strength though; she was definitely a strong woman. She was bold enough to face everybody at the banquet hall but I thought she was about to break down any moment. Then came Stephen, I knew his family was invited but he just couldn't resist coming over and rubbing more insult to my face. I almost lost my temper back then, I could have made a spectacle if Ambrose didn't intervene but I was more surprise at Elaine and how she handled herself. Stephen was cruel to her, yet she managed not to falter. Yes I admit she was strong but all strength had its limits. On our first night though, I couldn't help being mesmerized by her beauty, her auburn hair shone when it rested on her white robe, and her emerald green eyes glimmered even in the dark. It was my first time alone with a woman, I was nervous at first then I suddenly felt lonely, after I realized that physical attraction was never enough when there was nothing in the heart. After that night, I decided to sleep on a separate chamber.

    The next few days had not been easy. I spent most of my time avoiding Elaine and Andrew but I was glad she had her lessons which seemed to take most of her time so I didn't see her often. I thought she needed the lessons desperately if she was to keep up at being an Elite. The only time we saw each other was when I decide to dine at the dining room, and sometimes Lady Katherine would join but it didn't improve the mood. I spied on Elaine once when we were having our dinner, she seemed to have difficulty with which utensils to use that were laid on the table for her but she eventually improved over time, I guess the lessons were effective after all. Andrew had not joined us at the dining room ever since but he was not missed. I could also tell that the staff in the manor took a liking to Elaine, they seem always extra friendly with her. By then, everybody in Pinewood knew that a Beta was living as a Lady among the Elites, and I imagined the villagers talking about her when they gather at their own dinner tables, and I was certain some were enthusiastic of the news that someone from the lower station was elevated to the Elites. They may be celebrating but soon as time goes by, she would probably be forgotten, and then she would be just another pretentious Lady to them.

I was out on the grounds with Peter. Eager for the day to start, I wanted to get out of the manor because it had been a long time since I visited the villages once more and explored Pinewood. We made our way to the stables and I requested Mr. Witherson to ready the horses. While I waited, I observed that Protectors were arriving in groups all in their black and red uniforms. It was strange that they were here and Andrew never mentioned about them. We were about to leave on horseback through the main gate when two Protectors guarding the gate suddenly stopped us.

"Halt! No one is allowed to leave without authority from His Grace."

We reined our horses to a stop.

"This is Lord Curtis of House Bermule, brother to His Grace, let us through," Peter announced.

"My apologies my Lord but we have orders not to let anyone pass unless ordered by His Grace."

"What's going on here?" I demanded.

"I do not have clearance to answer that my Lord."

I had a feeling that the only one who had explanation to all this was Andrew. I turned the horse around frustrated that this had to happen today.

In the dining room, Lady Katherine decided to join us for dinner. The sound of our utensils can be heard as the three of us ate in silence. I usually preoccupied myself with my thoughts to make this more bearable. I was chewing my food when I suddenly choked so I cleared my throat and drank my wine. Lady Katherine and Elaine stared silently at me probably startled by my sudden sound.

"My apologies," I said, and then we continued eating as if nothing had happened.

Suddenly Andrew entered the dining room indiscreetly and decided to join us.

"I'm starving," he declared, and he sat on his chair at head of the table and Mr. Thistle immediately served him his first course then Andrew gobbled it down without paying much attention to us. I was staring at him, and knew that this was my only chance to ask but I was reluctant because I was not sure what mood he was in but I took the opportunity anyway.

"I was wondering brother if you could tell us what the Protectors are doing in Pinewood," I asked politely careful not to tread on his mood. The two Ladies glanced at me with uncertainty in their eyes.

"Them? It's nothing to be concerned about," he replied without looking up from his plate but I wasn't satisfied with his answer so I pursued further.

"If it's nothing to be concerned about then you could tell us why," I reluctantly asked.

"For protection and I don't want to hear another word about it," he commanded sounding annoyed.

There was more silence as he continued to eat.

"I have your leave then to visit the nearby villages," I

implied nervously.

"No, not this time," he declined.

"When then?" I insisted.

Andrew banged his hand on the table loudly that it startled the Ladies. There it was, I crossed the line again.

"When I say when. Why do you want to go there anyway?" he angrily questioned but I just sat there unmoved by his sudden outburst that sometimes I think I was getting used to it.

"Because they need help, and I promised that I would," I explained then I took a sip from my wine.

Andrew stopped eating then glared at me then I noticed Lady Katherine shifted nervously on her seat.

"You want to help?" he angrily asked, "Fine! Help all you want just as long as you get out of my way and stop annoying me. I'll give you leave if you bring your mate of yours with you and make her useful for once. Her sulking is getting on my nerves as well; the two of you could sulk together outside the manor."

That was not what I had in mind because I wanted to leave the manor to stay away from him and Elaine.

"The road is no place for a Lady brother," I reminded him trying to get out of this.

Andrew had an evil grin and retorted, "Either she comes along or no one leaves. Anyway, she is no real Lady so I am sure she is used to the inconvenience. I'll even put the two of you in charge of the farms if you like."

Nobody said a word.

Andrew smirked, "That's settled! So keep your mouth shut and don't bother me again."

Fine! I thought, if this was the only way for me to leave the manor then I would take it, and I just hoped Elaine won't be a nuisance.

ELAINE

I couldn't take another hour in that dining room. It was bad enough that I had to eat in silence but dining with Andrew was awful. Last night with him was the first and I feared would not be the last. I thought he was too proud to dine in my presence but I was wrong, he liked to lavish on the thought of torturing me. I preferred Lady Katherine's company though even if we hadn't exchange words since I arrived, but she gives warm smiles every time our path would cross. I thought at first she was like any other Elite Lady, vain and formal but she seemed nice. I was glad that Andrew didn't paid much attention to me yesterday but from what I saw, Curtis and Andrew were not the best of bothers one would hope for belonging to one family. The way they looked at each other, they loathed the other. I didn't know much about their family but it was not hard to decipher that they clearly had issues. Then Curtis brought up about going to the villages. I groaned deep inside when Andrew commanded that I should come along. It was not at the top of my list that I considered to be enjoyable. I wanted to refuse but I knew I couldn't, and then I hoped that leaving the manor was going to be more pleasant than staying here and do more of those lessons. Learning how to be a Lady was boring. My instructor, an old strict woman clearly a Delta who probably served many Lords and Ladies, even the Emperor and the Empress as she claims. She taught me nothing meaningful or significant except on how to be superficial, or how to act when dining in a formal setting and what proper utensils to use which according to her, tells a lot about a Lady especially on how she holds them. It was infuriating that you were being judged by how you hold a certain fork or knife. She would tap my hand with her stick whenever I did something improper or when she catches me rolling my eyes. She continued to instruct me on how to present myself if I run into another Lord or Lady or even Royalty. She would make a displeased face when I do or say something wrong. I knew she was not fond of me, and she thought I didn't deserve the promotion but I didn't care. One thing also that I was having a hard time adjusting was when the staff would bow or curtsied me; I tried telling them that it was not necessary but I think it became their habit so I left them to it.

      After the lessons, I sometimes would hide in one of the gardens or the library. Sometimes I would run into Miss Pattilyn who I always gladly welcomed her company. I was in the garden reading a book when Miss Pattilyn decided to join me. It was a warm day and we decided to spend it under the sun seated beside each other.

"That's a good book my Lady," she commended when she saw the book I placed down beside me.

"Oh it is," I agreed.

"Makes you feel that you are transported to the different places of the world."

We continued to sit in silence. I didn't know what came over me, maybe out of curiosity but I felt that I could trust Miss Pattilyn with anything so I asked her a peculiar question.

"Miss Pattilyn, I hope you don't mind me asking but do you know anyone else like me? A Beta turned Elite?" I hesitantly asked.

The question seem to caught her off guard but she contemplated for a moment then finally spoke, "I saw one my Lady when my previous Lady took me with her to visit a friend."

I grew excited, "Where is she now?"

"The Lady didn't live in the manor my Lady, she was also a friend visiting so my apologies if I don't know where she comes from and it was a long time ago, most people forgot who she is"

"Forgot who she is?" I asked confused.

She paused then continued, "Nobody could recall which one was she my Lady. I think she lost herself and renounced everything that she was and where she came from before her ascension. She decided to become one of the Elites instead. Everybody forgot that she was Beta, and over time they saw her as one of the Elites. I can recall her face though my Lady but I doubt if age did not change her and I am sorry I didn't get the chance to get her name."

"How come you knew she was Beta?" I asked curiously.

"My previous Lady once mentioned it to me my Lady."

"Who was your previous Lady?"

"Lady Loren, Lord Curtis' mother," she answered solemnly.

I sat speechless. Was that going to be my fate? To become the one thing that I hated the most. In years to come being surrounded by Elites, would I surrender to them? Would they finally break me? I could never forget mom and dad, I could never forget our little house in the suburbs of Coastal City but when you feel lonely for a long time, would I still have the courage to endure?

I felt Miss Pattilyn's gentle hand on my shoulder," Do not worry my Lady, she is not you and you are not her. You may have the same predicament but I am sure your minds are different and so are your hearts. Staying true to yourself would be your strongest foundation if ever you refuse to forget where you came from," she spoke such wise words that it gave me the comfort and the strength I needed.

"And by the way my Lady, please be patient with him," she warmly smiled changing the topic.

I looked at her confused what she was talking about.

"Lord Curtis, he too is lost my Lady," she shook her head, "He had gone through a lot especially the death of two parents at such a young age, our beloved Lord have never been himself since then, but he is a good Lord my Lady, he is just confused," she sadly revealed.

I didn't know about Curtis' parents but Miss Pattilyn's sincere sympathy for him, an Elite, made me regret of what I thought of him. It shed some light on why he was like this but I wasn't sure though. Andrew was his brother and he too lost both his parents yet I was not eager to be sympathetic with him. But I thought Miss Pattilyn with her kindness, deserved an assuring answer.

"I'll try," I promised.

It was late in the afternoon when I was walking along the hallway. I just came from the library returning a book when I came upon Mr. Logan and Andrew walking towards my direction. I was about to turn to a corner to avoid them but Andrew took notice and called my name. I stood my ground waiting for them. Andrew said something to Mr. Logan, then he bowed and left us. Andrew were all smiles when he approached.

"Join me for a walk?" he asked in a surprisingly friendly manner.

For me it was not a request so I obeyed unwillingly.

"Are you having fun yet?" he spoke while we took a stroll along the hallway but I couldn't read what his intention were, if it was made to be sarcastic or not.

"You know I could have changed your name when you got picked, but I didn't because I didn't see the point, it was not worth it so I took a gamble with you," he divulged.

We continued to take our time walking to nowhere in particular.

"But you had no idea how relieved I was when I first saw you, I thought we were going to be stuck with some ordinary and plain commoner," he chuckled then he continued, "I would have been easily be bored with you, but you're not going to be boring are you?"

I didn't answer right away. I didn't know if he expected me to say something about that but he was waiting for a reply.

"I'll do my best not to be," I reluctantly obliged.

"Good! I'd expect the same obedience when the time comes when I have use of you."

"I beg your pardon?" I suddenly felt uncomfortable.

He smiled looking amused, "Did you think that I was only doing this for my entertainment? I admit that I was having so much fun with everybody's reaction but I also brought you here for the attention. You're like an exotic pet, a distraction for the bored Elites. Lords and Ladies would call on me because of their curiosity of you. They all want to take a look at you, like a sheep in a cage, they'd be wondering how the low birth acts and lives especially when thrust among lions."

He suddenly stopped walking then stepped in front of me. He held my hair, touching the ends, and stared at me, "It was supposed to be a joke intended for Curtis but I feel that I am doing him a favor instead," he sighed and came close, too close to my face as he whispered something in my ear, "Maybe someday you'd return the favor in my private bed chamber."

My eyes widened in horror. No words could ever express what I felt after his indecency. I was powerless and hopeless. His disturbing words echoed in my ears and shook my inner core.

Andrew continued to stare at me then sneered, "It was nice talking to you, we should do this again," and with that he walked away leaving me in shock. Adultery was against the law, even the thought of it was punishable by death. I could report him but would it do any good? He was the Duke of Pinewood, it was my words against his. He could twist my words and have me arrested instead for treason. I was a plaything for these people, just here for their amusement and if I did something about it, it would be their ultimate entertainment. I felt like crying and I wanted to run away for good but where would I go? Who would save me?

I felt terrible the next day. I didn't get any sleep; what Andrew said still rang in my head, and I was so homesick. I wanted to go home so badly to mom and dad, and lay in my own room where I felt most safe. This room, this manor, would never be called my home. I chose to stay in my chambers deliberately missing my morning lessons. A maid knocked on my door to wake me up but I told her that I wish not to be disturbed again which she obliged without any question. I continued to lie on my bed, even refusing to eat. There was another knock, this time it was one of the footman. He announced from outside the door that Lord Curtis had summoned me to his private office. I wanted to refuse; I didn't want to see anyone including him but I knew I couldn't decline so I told the footman that I would be right out. The footman took me to a room and he knocked at the door where I heard Curtis' voice say come in. The footman opened the door for me then closed it when I was in. The office had a wooden desk at the center and two leather seats in front of it. Curtis was seated in his large leather chair behind the desk. There were books and maps cluttered at a nearby table, and a window looking out the grounds of the manor. A young man was standing beside the desk with his hands behind his back, he was lean and timid. Curtis stood from his chair, "Please have a seat my Lady," he gestured me to the chairs in front. I made myself comfortable in one of them. He did the same on his seat and placed his elbows on the table.

"I summoned you because we will be leaving for the Frist Village tomorrow at dawn and Peter here," he glanced at the young man standing, "will brief you of our travels. Peter you may begin."

"Thank you my Lord. My Lady," Peter bowed then continued, "I hope you won't mind starting our day tomorrow at a very early time since we want to be back here before night fall."

I sat there patiently waiting for him to continue.

"It is going to be a hot day tomorrow my Lady but not to worry you will be riding in one of our close carriage to keep you from the sun."

"No," I objected.

"No? My Lady," Peter stuttered.

"I rather ride on horseback," I firmly declared.

"My Lady, I am sorry but you would be more comfortable on a carriage, and besides riding on horseback wearing a dress would be difficult my Lady," Peter nervously explained.

"Then I would wear my riding clothes which is more practical."

Peter grew concern and glanced at Curtis' direction as if asking for his help to persuade me to do otherwise but Curtis only remained silent.

"But my Lady, an Elite Lady should never wear pants when seen by the public," Peter anxiously continued.

"But I am no Elite nor a Lady am I?" I said in a stern voice.

He had difficulty responding to the question. He was clearly struggling with me. He glanced at Curtis again waiting for an objection from him but he continued to patiently listen without saying a word.

Convinced that Curtis had no problem or objection with my request, Peter conceded, "Whatever my Lady wants, I am obliged to follow."

I was smiling inside over the victory.

"And lastly my Lady, the village we will be visiting is called the First Village in Eastwood. It's one of the largest village in Pinewood. When we arrive there, you are not required to talk or socialize with the villagers if you do not wish to my Lady," Peter added.

Like any other proper Elite was expected to do. Peter must have thought I was like them, proud and too good for the lower station but I didn't want to argue with him anymore especially since he was only doing his job so I nodded to acknowledge.

Curtis leaned on his chair and finally spoke, "Now that we're done, do you have any questions?"

I wanted to confide in him about what happened yesterday because I really needed someone to talk to and I thought maybe he could help but I changed my mind, he was his brother, his brother's blood runs through him as well, and why would he help me? He was the same as them; only difference was that he was stuck with me. Does he regard me as a plaything too? Or probably a nuisance that he had to endure for their entertainment. Miss Pattilyn may have sympathy for him and I gave my word that I would try to be patient. I could give him my sympathy, sympathy that he had a brother much worse than him.

CHAPTER 6: FIRST VILLAGE

CURTIS

    The air was still cool as the sun had not yet risen. I wanted an early start to have more time to enjoy the fresh air and scenery and a change of pace was what I needed. Peter and I were at the stables first getting ready when Elaine arrived wearing beige coat and pants, and high black boots and with her hair down. I was use to her wearing her dresses in the manor but her riding clothes extremely suited her as well. I hope she would keep up I thought. I recalled when she insisted on going horseback instead of riding a carriage. She was stubborn and persistent but I didn't care, and she can do what she wanted as long as she didn't spoil this for me. Our horses were ready and Peter tried to assist Elaine in climbing her white horse but clearly she didn't need any help after all. We started for the gate with me leading the way and Peter taking the rear. The Protectors guarding let us through this time without any questions. Shortly when we left the manor, the sun began to slowly appear over the horizon. The sky changed its color from dark to a tinged of orange. It was time for the heavens to wake up and I was there as it all unfolded. We were taking our time riding in a slow pace. I felt alone and free out here, and finally drowning out the noises in my head, a refreshing feeling that I hadn't felt for a while. As we continued to ride, I realized that Elaine and Peter were riding side by side behind as she asked him questions about Pinewood. It sounded like she was enjoying herself and was curious of the land and Peter was happy to answer. I rode ahead of them until we neared Greendale forest.

"Is that the forest you were talking about?" Elaine inquired.

"Yes my Lady, it's the largest in Pinewood," Peter responded.

"This must be the forest we passed when I flew over here."

"It was my Lady."

"There must be all kinds of creatures in there. Are we going through?" she excitedly asked.

"No my Lady, we are going around it."

"But why? Isn't it faster to go through?"

"Well my Lady, it's not safe through these woods. It is better if we go around instead."

"Nonsense, it's daytime, the dangers out here are probably the same as in there."

Elaine and Peter continued bickering; she insists on going through while he tries to convince her otherwise. It got to the point that it got annoying so I turned my horse to face them that it made their own horses stop.

"Look, you two can say what you want but I decide where we go, and I chose to go around it and that would be the end of it," I suddenly blurted frustrated and they were startled by my sudden outburst. Elaine was frowning and Peter looked guilty then I turned my horse back around and resumed our journey. We rode in silence at last but I suddenly regretted what I just said to them. I should had said it more nicely but it was too late for that, so I tried to forget about it.

It took us longer to go around Greendale forest but when we reached the other side, we took a break under a shade of tree as the sun was up. I sat on the trunk while Peter gave the horses water. I glanced at who Elaine decided to rest on the other tree not far from where I was.

She took off her coat and laid it down beside her, revealing a white long sleeve fitted collared shirt that she wore underneath. She took a sip of her water and seemed to prefer being left alone.

We were on the road again and the day started to get warmer. I picked up the pace and Elaine and Peter did the same as they continued to follow. We were finally at the fields of the First Village and the villagers took notice as we approached. They were all smiles and bowed and children started following us. Some were waving happily and some came towards our direction excitedly. They were not like this when I came I thought; it must be Elaine they were excited to see. The anticipated visit stirred the villagers that day and Mr. Conolly was waiting for us at the side of the road when we reached his house. Sure enough when we climbed down from our horses, a crowd started to form around Elaine, all were smiling, curious and happy that she came. She smiled widely at them in return and was friendly to all.

"Forgive me my Lord," Mr. Conolly apologized as he approached me and bowed and smiled, "but they have been waiting to see her since you sent word that you would come with the Lady. We never had a Lady visit here before."

"No need to apologize," I smiled back.

"The Lady has become extremely popular among us common folks my Lord and I see that the rumors of her beauty are all true."

I was watching her and the villagers around. They all looked so happy and mesmerized by her like a worshipper to a deity, and in return she was genuinely delighted to be with them. She spoke to them and didn't even mind their proximity. She laughed and smiled as they talked to her; it was then that I realized that she became a whole different person to me, I have never seen her like this. Her elation made me feel like it was the first time I saw her, and her cheerfulness made her eyes sparkle more and I couldn't help feel that I was starting to be drawn to it. Was there something that I saw in her now that I didn't back then? I waited for her patiently at the sides while she at the center of the crowd where she radiantly stood out, until Mr. Conolly decided to break it off and disperse the villagers.

"Alright folks, let the Lady have her rest, she's tired from her journey," he declared cheerfully going towards Elaine while fighting his way through the crowd.

"My Lady," he bowed, "I am Mr. James Conolly, in charge of this village. Let me welcome you to our humble home. We are so honored that you decide to grace us with your presence," he happily greeted.

Elaine gleamed, "The pleasure is mine Mr. Conolly, I am happy to be here and meet these wonderful people."

Mr. Conolly smiled in return, "Shall we my Lady?" he guided her to the house.

The villagers gave way for them to pass as they move towards the house while I followed. Mrs. Conolly and Hannah were already waiting for us and were ecstatic when we joined them. They curtsied and Hannah couldn't contain herself that she was jumping with excitement and gave Elaine a gentle hug. Elaine was delightfully surprised then hugged her in return and smiled and laughed at her reaction. Hannah was praising her and she showered her with adoration and it was obvious that Elaine was not used to it that I noticed her face turned bright red. Mr. Conolly intervene once again, "Okay Hannah, that's enough," he kindly told her and she obliged but continued staring at Elaine with fondness. We sat at their dining table and the food were more carefully prepared than the last time I was here but just as delicious, and it was more like a feast with more variety. The Conolly seemed very eager to have us in their home. We were talking about their life in the village, the neighbors, and his family. They laughed at Mr. Conolly's embarrassing moments that he shared. They all looked happy that sitting here made me forget that I was their Lord. This must be what it felt like to belong to a family who cared and loved one another. They might be a family of meager wealth but they looked like they already had everything. The meal was more than satisfactory and I complimented the family. We moved to the living room after we had our meal. The three women lead the way, and I was about to follow when I overheard whispers and it sounded that it came from Mr. Conolly and Peter who remained at the kitchen.

"We can trust him, I know I do," Peter whispered.

"I don't know…. he is a Lord, an Elite," Mr. Conolly spoke in a low voice.

"But he can help us."

"Shhh.. let me think about it. We can talk about this some other time."

I had no clue what they were talking about but whatever they were referring to, I was sure it was of secrecy. I hurriedly went to the living room when I heard their footsteps coming then we were all gathered at the living room drinking coffee talking about the farms when Mr. Conolly brought up the topic about his horse limping.

"I could take a look at him if you want," Elaine offered willingly.

We were taken off guard by her statement. I was puzzled what she meant then Elaine became aware of our surprised look and explained, "Oh I was an animal doctor before I came to Pinewood."

Mr. Conolly chuckled, "Are you sure my Lady? It would be of great help."

"It's not a problem at all."

Elaine and I followed Mr. Conolly to his barn where he kept his horse. He took out the brown horse that was smaller than what we had at the manor from its stable, and it was indeed limping. Elaine came over and stroked the horse trying to calm it down, and then she gently checked its knees and hooves while we silently watched. When she was at the right front leg, she bent down and slowly raised it to inspect underneath the hoof.

"You poor boy," she spoke with pity.

"Have you found anything wrong my Lady?" Mr. Conolly asked with a hint of concern in his voice.

"Yes, see here?" she pointed underneath the hoof that she raised, "there's an abscess forming near the shoe that is what's causing the limp but don't worry, the infection has not spread yet," she gently released the horse's leg then stood up and faced Mr. Conolly, "Just soak the infected hoof daily with warm water and lots of salt then place a bandage over it to keep it clean. Do this until the inflammation will be gone then he'll be fine."

Mr. Conolly was extremely grateful, "Thank you, Thank you my Lady you have no idea how much this means to us."

"I'm happy to be of help," Elaine spoke chuckling.

I was surprised and impressed by her. I didn't know what she did before she came to Pinewood but I could tell that she was good at her job. This was a side of her that I was unaware of and it made me curious who she really was before she came to Pinewood. Elaine and Mr. Connoly continued to talk while we stood there at the barn when there was a sudden commotion in the village and we went hurriedly outside to investigate. The villagers were panicking as groups of Protectors stormed the village and tried to secure the area while pushing villagers along the way. Mr. Conolly was running towards the disturbance and went to a Protector with gray hair who was the only one not wearing a helmet, and his badge told me that he was a commanding officer. I could hear from a distance Mr. Conolly asking him for an explanation but the officer ignored him, and after much begging, the officer suddenly pushed aside Mr. Conolly with force that he fell on the ground then he suddenly pointed his firearm at Mr. Conolly. Mrs. Conolly screamed from the house and was about to run towards her mate but Hannah stopped her just in time. I felt the need to intervene and help them so I ran towards Mr. Conolly and Elaine followed me not far behind.

"What is the meaning of this?" I shouted demanding an explanation.

The officer looked at me while still pointing his firearm at Mr. Conolly who was on the ground sweating and terrified.

"Put your gun down and let him up!" I commanded.

The officer with his stern face stared at me unimpressed, "And who are you to give such an order?"

I glared back at him not intimidated, "Lord Curtis from the House of Bermule."

He continued to stare still unaffected, "I have orders to search these areas."

"Who gave the orders?" I strongly asked.

"From the Emperor. We received reports that Defiers

are here in the area."

"I assure you that there are no rebels around here only farmers who would have gladly cooperated so let him up," I spoke strongly referring to the release of Mr. Conolly.

The Protector was hesitant for a minute and was still glaring at me, probably testing me, and then he finally pointed his firearm away and inserted it to his side buckle. Peter who was suddenly appeared helped Mr. Conolly up on his feet.

"I would have to ask you to leave this village immediately," I ordered sternly.

"You do not have the authority to give such order," he objected without fear.

"I am an Elite, that is authority enough," I walked towards him and stared at him coldly in the eye unhinged, "I am Lord here, born having the right to rule this land like my forefathers. Who are you to tell me otherwise?" I continued threatening him. To tell the truth, the Duke was the ruler of these lands not a Lord like me but I still outrank this officer though. He stood his ground and the way he stared, it seems that he had no intention of taking any orders from me. I was secretly hoping that he would not do anything that would aggravate the situation when out of nowhere Elaine stood beside me and spoke with such conviction to the Protector that it rattled me, "Enough! How dare you frighten these innocent women and children. Is that any way the Empire treats its citizens?!"

The officer shifted his stare at Elaine. Both of them were determined not to falter in front of the other then I feared for her, she could be arrested but surprisingly he yielded to her.

"Sergeant," he spoke to the Protector beside him.

"Yes Captain Furlong?" the sergeant responded.

"Tell the men we are done here for now," he commanded.

"Right away sir," the sergeant obeyed and instructed the rest of his group to move out.

"My Lord," Captain Furlong nodded and took his leave with no traces of remorse or fear. The Protectors started to load to their transport then eventually left.

"They'll be back my Lord, probably with more troops," Mr. Conolly sadly declared.

"Why do you say that?" I asked worried.

"It's not only here my Lord, they've been patrolling everywhere lately."

It was not a good sign that the Protectors were here, and the Captain mentioned the Defiers were at Pinewood, the Empire had been hunting these rebels since their existence was made known but not like this before, not this many and with such force.

    We were on our way back to the manor. I lead the way again not in a hurry to return. The trees were still this time with no wind to gracefully dance with them. Everything remained peaceful but when I glanced behind, Elaine was not her happy self since we left the village. She remained as distant like before but I didn't find her at fault then I suddenly felt sorry for her, I admit that I was not the most favorable companion and the place we were returning was not exactly something we were looking forward to. No one spoke a word the whole time even when we took a rest under the shade of the trees. I took out the bread wrapped in clean cloth that Mrs. Conolly gave us for the journey back. I went over to where Elaine was sitting a few meters away. I was holding the cloth with the bread and sat beside not far from her. She ignored me when I approached as we sat there watching the horizon in front of us.

"I apologize for my behavior this morning, I didn't know what came over me," I reluctantly apologized not sure what she thought of it.

I saw her surprised expression and uneasiness when I spoke to her but she continued to look forward.

"It doesn't matter," she finally muttered devoid of any happiness while refusing to look at me.

I unwrapped the cloth and broke the bread into two and gave her the other half. She glanced at it hesitantly but accepted it and took a little bites. I stood up and left her alone which I thought she needed. I went over to Peter who was letting the horse graze and gave him the other half which he gladly accepted.

It was late in the afternoon when we arrived at the manor. Peter brought back the horses to the stables.

"I'm going to see my brother," I stated to Elaine.

"Let me come with you," she hurriedly blurted.

Her words startled me, maybe because it was our first conversation as I stared at her, "Why?"

"I know what you're going to ask him and I need to know as well."

I was hesitant and became worried for her but I was not going to argue because she deserves to know, so I nodded.

We found Andrew in his private office sitting behind his desk. I knocked and we entered his office. He was surprised to see us but his face lit up in an amusing way.

"Just got back from your journey?" he asked grinning.

I stood in front of him while Elaine decided to stay silently in a corner far away from Andrew.

"I didn't come here for small talks Andrew. The Protectors were at the First Village wreaking havoc, did you know anything about this?" I spoke directly to the point.

Andrew was calm and ignored the question then he said, "This is a conversation for men, not with a Lady present," he briefly glanced at Elaine who stood at the corner.

"As if her presence matters to you, and she was there, she saw everything," I said irritated by his stalling.

He sighed then leaned on his desk, "Fine! Yes I knew about them. They were sent here to search for the Defiers and were ordered to use strict measures to find them since report of their activity in Pinewood were discovered."

"Do they know why Defiers are here in Pinewood?"

"No official reports yet but they assume these rebels are planning an attack."

"But why?" I asked aghast.

Andrew shrugged looking annoyed, "Who knows!"

"But why do the Protectors need to use such force?"

"These Defiers could be anywhere or anyone. Fear is the only way to uncover them and if force is necessary they should condone it," he spoke firmly with such belief to his own words.

What he said felt wrong. I knew these Defiers were dangerous but the innocent didn't need to be harm for their sake.

"Curtis, I have been doing this longer than you. Now leave me and let me rule Pinewood," he stated dismissing us not wanting to hear another word. I left Andrew but before I could reach the door I briefly glanced at Elaine and saw her look of disappointment and it was troubling me that I felt that I should had done more but I was overpowered by Andrew. Her opinion didn't matter to me before, but I didn't understand why it bothered me then.

The Protectors continued to patrol Pinewood and the manor, and Andrew became more preoccupied since their arrival. He did put me in charge of the farms so I kept myself busy. I entered my private office and as I approached my desk, I found a book placed in the middle, it was odd because I couldn't recall putting it there. As I took the book away, a note fell on my desk, and I was puzzled where it came from. I slowly unfolded it and an unfamiliar handwriting was written saying *'Come to the Greendale forest when the sun is at its highest and look for me where you saw the rabbit.'* I looked around the room searching if the one who left this was still inside but there was just silence. I was bewildered and the note seemed vague and suspicious and there was no name or place stating where it came from. And how come he knew about the rabbit I saw at Greendale? It was only Peter who was with me that day. Could Peter have sent this? So I rang for Mr. Thistle, thinking he might know who was in my office.

"My apologies my Lord but I did not order any messages to be delivered in your office today," Mr. Thistle explained when he arrived at my office.

I sat on my chair contemplating who could have.

"Could you send Peter here to my office Mr. Thistle?" I requested.

"At once my Lord," he obliged bowed and left.

A few moments later, there was a soft knock at my door and I called out to whoever it was to enter. The door opened and Peter appeared.

"You send for me my Lord?"

I showed him the note and he looked as puzzled as I

was as he entered the office.

"Do you know anything about this?" I asked as I gave the note to him to read.

"No my Lord," Peter answered shaking his head.

I leaned in my chair deep in thought. My curiosity was killing me. I wanted to know what this mysterious sender wanted from me but this could be a trap of some sort to lure a Lord. But who would want to trap me? I had no power unlike Andrew. But what was there to lose if I go? For all I knew this sender maybe in need of my help. I looked up to Peter. I trusted him so there was no reason to go alone.

"I'm going and you're coming with me," I declared to Peter.

His face turned pale, "I beg your pardon my Lord but this could be dangerous, we don't know who send you this letter.

"I know that's why you're coming with me."

Peter looked defeated and he knew he could not decline my command.

"Very well my Lord," he accepted unwillingly.

"Good! Ready the horses then and tell no one."

It was almost midday when we set out for Greendale. We were on our horses on a hot day then we arrived at the forest and I pull the reins of my horse to a stop before we proceeded.

"Are you sure about this my Lord?" Peter asked sounding very worried and reluctant.

I didn't answer; instead I reined my horse to move forward into the forest and Peter did the same. We slowly passed through giant trees following the road trying to remember where I last saw the rabbit. It was cooler inside the forest since it was hard for the sun to penetrate through. We were looking around cautiously for any signs of danger or a life form. Then I finally stopped at a familiar place.

"This is it," I announced. I stared into the trees searching if anybody was hiding behind them. We climbed down from our horses and waited patiently. The forest was quiet except the sounds of a few birds and unknown critters. We waited some more but no one came.

"Maybe we should go my Lord," Peter suggested and I sensed his apprehensiveness.

I looked around searching between the trees one more time. Convinced that no one was coming, I was about to ride on my horse when I heard a voice.

"I wasn't expecting you to come," said a deep voice from somewhere among the trees.

I turned around startled, "Show yourself!" I demanded searching where the voice came from.

A dark figure came out from behind one of the trees. It was hard to see who it was hiding among the shadows but as he appeared stepping out into the light I saw that he was a large tall man of strong built, he had a short white hair and he looked like someone of age yet his strength never left him. I stared at him then I recalled who he was as he stood in front of me, "You were at the bar at Moors town," I stated full of certainty.

The mysterious man grinned and spoke in his deep husky voice, "Glad that you remembered."

"You were following us the first time I was here," I observed.

"I heard about the young Lord that came home."

"Who are you?"

"I am called Olfren," he bowed slightly.

"Well Olfren, how did you manage to sneak a message

to my office without being detected?"

"I have my ways," he gave a mischievous smile.

I continued to stare at him, gauging him what kind of man he was, "You got my attention so what do you want?" I firmly asked.

"I am here to offer redemption."

He was playing tricks with me, his vague answers only made me distrust him more.

"If you continue to answer like that then I have no choice but to leave you," I threatened annoyed by his lack of exactness.

He stared at me searching for any clue of how serious I was before he explained.

"Long before you came back to Pinewood, James Conolly reached out to us asking for help about something that was happening here," he paused then continued, "We came to investigate and we found out that everything he claimed were true."

I stared silently at him puzzled but waited patiently for him to continue.

"The Duke of Pinewood found great wealth in his Steel Plants that he built more. The Steel plants required more people to run it but most of the villagers of Pinewood were farmers, contented with their lives on the fields, where they can enjoy their produce at the same time sell it for a fair price which was more than what a steel worker was earning," he paused before he continued, "With the lack of manpower, the Duke decided to force villagers to work there. At first they were given meager wages but soon after more Plants were built, more people were needed and so more of them refused. The Duke then ordered his guards to round up innocent villagers and accused them of a crime they didn't commit, even if you simply displeased the Duke you were accused, and instead of going to prison, they were sent to the plants to work with no wages, only food and water. If they refuse to work, they will be tortured or one of their family would be."

"I couldn't believe what I just heard. That something like that could ever happen here in a peaceful place like Pinewood. I knew Andrew was terrible but not like this, my own brother. I was in shock and appalled that he would permit slavery. It was illegal and had been abolished in the Empire for a very long time.

"No this can't be true," I denied astounded and was sadly shaking my head.

"Believe me I also wished it wasn't."

"Does the Empire know?"

Olfren shook his head, "We do not know yet but we know that other Dukes and some Lords do."

"Yet they did nothing?" I said sounding disgusted.

"They can't because some of them are doing it themselves."

"What??" I was in shock.

"We are at the pinnacle of time where wealth means more power, and with more power, more people has to suffer."

"But I really thought Andrew had supported the farms."

"Lies! The Duke is slowly demolishing farming in Pinewood especially when Steel is more lucrative for him," he reported.

"But those people, held against their will......" I had the loss for words.

"Are suffering unless you help us."

"Me?" I spoke not expecting his words.

Olfren nodded, "Who better to help the people of Pinewood than its Lord, and James Conolly told us that we can trust you."

I didn't get the sense of what he was saying. Yes I was a Lord but I have no power over Andrew and if I do help then get caught, it would mean my life. The Lord who betrayed his own Duke, nothing like that had ever happened before. I would be the destruction of my own family but if I didn't do anything, I will be the destruction of Pinewood as well.

"Look," Olfren suddenly spoke calmly, "I do not expect you to answer right away. Take time to think about it until it sinks in but remember your people are suffering, and the longer we do nothing the more difficult it would be especially with the Protectors around."

It became suddenly clear to me when I stared directly at Olfren, "You are one of them, a Defier," I spoke in a manner that I discovered something significant.

He grinned, "You catch on pretty quick."

"So this is what you're doing here? To stop the slavery?"

"Yes and among others. What we have here in Pinewood is just a part of a larger picture. The Defiers was created for a much greater cause that you probably can't fathomed at the moment, but that story would be for another time and I am not the best person to tell it. When the time comes that you decide to help us, then we'll talk again."

"If I do decide to help, what do you need of me?"

"Your support. We need access and your connections."

I just stood there saying nothing suddenly feeling a heavy burden was placed upon my shoulders.

"The day has been long and I feel that our time here is

done. We need to leave before someone might notice us," I suddenly declared.

I was on my horse when Olfren suddenly took hold of my reigns when he spoke to me with urgency, "Promise me that you will say nothing to anyone about what happened here or we both will be in trouble."

I stared down at him and said, "I give you my word."

Olfren finally relaxed his grip on the reigns.

"And oh nice job at the First Village, James Conolly told me what happened and what you did, but people are talking more about your Lady and how she saved the villagers from the Protectors. She's very popular now among the Betas and Omegas. Too bad their stories left you out of it," he chuckled and went off his separate way.

CHAPTER 7: REVELATIONS

ELAINE

    I was at the library searching for a book that would catch my eye. I wanted to spend the day outside but it was getting too hot lately. My lessons finally ended and my teacher had a look of defeat on her when she told me that she had done the best she could. I was relieved when she said it was over, and then I would not see her ever again. I was slowly walking among the bookshelves and there were books about The Great War, The Conquest of Fortis, Yuvaika: The Strong and The Wise, and some more books about history, the world, and the Empire, and more books about other different Empires, and books documenting great men and women and their accomplishments that affected the lives of millions while here I was, sulking most of the time, hating what my life had become. During my visit at the First Village though was when I felt my true self again. It was a lovely release, and I felt once again that I belonged. I was not expecting to enjoy the visit but I was completely delighted by their warm welcome. It was refreshing talking to them where I would not be judged by my actions or words. The villagers were even amused when I told them to call me by name instead of my Lady and when I told them not to bow, I saw in their faces that they were bewildered by my words but they had the widest smile after. They thought of me a real Lady but truly I was just like them. I may have dressed the part of an Elite but I was still Elaine Gertrue of Coastal City. When the Protectors arrived at the village, my heart broke when I saw how terrified the villagers were. Curtis surprised me though when he defended Mr. Conolly. I honestly thought he was just going to stand there and watch but I didn't expect him to run towards Mr. Conolly when the Captain pointed his firearm at him. I was afraid that day that someone was going to get hurt especially the way how Curtis and the Captain exchanged words. That was when I felt the need to intervene, and I was scared at first but I needed to do something before it got out of hand, and I was relieved when the Captain finally conceded. Curtis and I barely spoke again after that day and I didn't mind, but I was grateful for what he did for Mr. Conolly.

 I continued my search when I came upon a green book that seemed old but was still in good condition. I glanced at the words written in gold on the spine and it read The History of Pinewood. I took it out from the shelf, and I saw the seal of the House of Bermule which was a tree painted with gold on the cover. I placed the book on the table nearby and I sat down a chair and opened it. The paper had a hint yellow discoloration as time got hold of it but the words written were still readable. I read through the first few pages; it dated back to its ancestry during the time of the very first Emperor Fortis. Lord Desmond was brother to the Emperor and closest confidant; he was the crucial piece to the Emperor's army with his exceptional talent in military tactics. He won the Battle of Pinewood that it temporarily crippled Yuvaika's forces. When peace finally came, he was one of the Emperor's loyal supporters to be granted a Dukedom by the Emperor and he was given one of the largest lands which was Pinewood. Lord Desmond then took a mate from one of Yuvaika's powerful allies, and he made Bermule the name of his House. Pinewood flourished under his rule, his kindness and his sense of justice made him beloved to the people. Farming and agriculture was their main source of wealth and Pinewood had an abundance of it. I flipped through the pages and came upon a family tree. Andrew and Curtis' names were at the bottom and on top of it was the name of their parents Lord Triston and Lady Loren. I had seen their names somewhere before along the hallway below a portrait but I didn't know that they were Curtis' mother and father. I closed the book and returned it. That was enough history for today.

I made my way through the corridors and decided to go to the portrait where I saw the names. I found them not far from the library near the balcony overlooking the gardens. Lord Triston's portrait looked almost exactly like Andrew while Lady Loren was beautiful and she had this elegance in her, her white skin glowed against the dark blue gown that she wore, and her blue eyes were astonishing as they resonated on the painting, her long black wavy curls shone as they flowed almost to her waist. She looked like Curtis except that she was happy with her enchanting smile. I couldn't help but be captivated by her. I was admiring the portrait when a voice suddenly interrupted me.

"She's beautiful wasn't she my Lady?"

I looked around startled and I saw Miss Pattilyn standing behind me.

"Yes she was," I smiled.

Miss Pattilyn then stood beside me and was admiring the portrait, "It's a shame that she's gone."

"How did she die?" I asked respectfully.

Miss Pattilyn sighed, "A terrible accident my Lady while on horseback riding," she replied sadly, "The entire household cried when she had passed, and she was so loved," she added solemnly.

We stood there in silence for a while looking at the painting.

"But no one was devastated as Lord Curtis. He was only a child when she passed. They were very close and he was her favorite. He never cried in public though but I knew he was when he was alone behind closed doors," I could sense that this was hard for Miss Pattilyn to talk about.

It was hard for me to imagine losing a mother and father. I would be destroyed too if I lost mom and dad, I wouldn't know what to do if that would happen then I suddenly felt sorry for Curtis. What could have been going through his mind losing a mother and father while he was still a child? The thought of it raised the hairs on my skin.

"Oh look at the time! My apologies my Lady but I have things to do. I should take my leave," Miss Pattilyn hurriedly spoke then curtsied and left after she gave me a warm smile.

I continued roaming the huge hallway after Miss Pattiyln left. I was about to turn a corner when I heard something broke. It sounded like it came from just ahead and sure enough when I turned, I saw a little girl with brown curly long hair that shone like velvet standing over something that was broken on the floor. She saw me and was suddenly frightened then I hurriedly went to where she was.

"Are you hurt?" I asked concerned as I knelt before her. She shook her head and tears started to fill her eyes.

"It's okay don't cry," I comforted her while gently placing a hand on her shoulder, "Don't worry I won't tell anyone, it will be our little secret," I assured her smiling.

She smiled in return and wiped her tears.

"What's your name?" I softly asked smiling.

"Kat," she responded smiling shyly.

She must be Katherine and Andrew's daughter; she resembles so much of her mother.

"Well Kat, I'm Elaine but you can call me Ellie. Nice to meet you," I extended my hand to her and we playfully shook while giggling.

"That will also be our little secret, nobody knows I'm Ellie but you can call me that when it's just the two of us, deal?" I said teasingly.

"Deal!" she nodded cheerfully and we continued to giggle.

I entered the dining room not looking forward to this. Katherine and Curtis were already there and it looked like they had just began eating. Katherine smiled when she saw me approaching and I smiled in return. Curtis was seated across from her and didn't saw me coming. He briefly glanced at me when I took my seat beside him but he did not show any reaction. I was getting used to this were we ignore each other. I ate in silence when the footman served my first course. I could never get used to the food here, everything was delicious and extravagant, and every night if I decide to dine in this room, the food was always different and there were more than one course; unlike back home when sometimes we would only have leftovers from the night before. I felt guilty whenever I ate these lavish meals when mom and dad back home only ate one type of food each meal. I was startled when the door suddenly burst open. It was Andrew and I could see that he was in his foul mood. He sat on his chair grumping, and then Mr. Thistle hurriedly placed his first course in front of him. Andrew angrily waved at Mr. Thistle signaling him that he didn't want it, so Mr. Thistle took it away then served the second course which Andrew didn't object. He was cutting through the meat angrily then gave up and threw his knife and fork at his plate which clanged in the silent room.

"When I catch those Defiers, they're going to regret coming here," Andrew angrily declared to no one in particular. We stopped eating and sat silently not daring to look at him.

"You know what they did?! They attacked one of the trucks," he shouted furiously venting his anger to no one. He grabbed his glass and drank the wine from it.

"And those fools," he angrily continued in a low voice, "those villagers harboring these rebels. Ungrateful people. They complain about everything and whine like little children but when they need help, they'll come running to me. No sense of loyalty whatsoever."

I didn't know what came over me that night but maybe I was tired of him, tired of how he felt so entitled that he can do or say anything as he pleases, and I was frustrated that he always got his way.

"Maybe if you were good to them they would be," I mockingly muttered under my breath while I took a sip from my wine.

I saw Katherine's jaws dropped and her eyes were wide opened in horror. Curtis stared at me frozen on his chair similarly shocked. They heard me.

"What did you just say?" Andrew emphasized his every word when he asked while his fury started to grow on his face.

I didn't answer and pretended I said nothing. Andrew continued to stare at me full of hatred then he drank all of his wine in one gulp and wiped his mouth with the back of his hand, then a footman hurriedly refilled it.

"I received another message from your father last

week requesting an audience with me," Andrew said nonchalantly changing the topic, "Of course I didn't allow it so I sent my lawyer instead."

I sat there listening anticipating his next words.

"You know what he wanted? He begged to see his daughter because they miss her so much," he taunted with an evil grin, "and I responded to him that the only time that you will ever get to see your daughter is when you are lying on your bed…. dry…. wrinkled…. worn out…. and unrecognizable, and by that time, you would have forgotten her as your mind starts to deteriorate into nothing, and she will also forget about you as she becomes a high class Lady too good to be seen by the likes of you."

Every part me started to scream as the fire of rage swept through every inch of my being. I was overwhelmed, blinded, by such fury that I might lose myself.

"How dare you," I said slowly, loathing, and every word was drowning in hate.

Andrew let out a sinister laugh, loud and menacing, "Face it! Here you are enjoying every pleasures I have to offer, my food, the soft bed, my servants, and the fine clothes. Sooner or later you can't live without it, you'd probably be craving for it just like any other Lady. You should be grateful that you're living what every Beta, Omega, or even an Alpha can only dream of while the rest of your friends and family are rotting their lives away working."

I could feel the tears fall down my cheeks. I wanted to say something back and I wanted to hurt him so bad.

"Trust me, you'll get used to being an Elite that you'll forget what your life was like before all this. Your past ends here and there is nothing you can do about it," Andrew sneered and raised his glass making a toast at my direction. It was getting harder to breath, I felt a lump in my throat as tears started to fall. I was suffocating. I felt myself falling, losing control. I wanted more than ever to get away from this place. Escape and never come back. What they would do to me didn't matter anymore; so I did what I felt was right, I suddenly stood up from where I sat then ran away as fast as I could. I didn't know where my feet were taking me as I crossed the hallway until I reached the back door. I hurriedly opened it then ran outside into the cool night. I passed through the gardens almost running out of breath, and then the large garage until I finally reached the stables. I stopped outside and nobody was there. I was panting and sobbing at the same time in the cold night air. I was frantically looking around from where I stood, not knowing what to do or where to go. My hands were trembling, my knees were starting to falter, and my eyes were blurred as the tears continued to fall. I was startled when I heard a horse neighed loudly behind me. I turned around and saw a dark figure riding a large black horse. As the horse trotted towards me, the moonlight shone on the rider who sat on the horse with no saddle or bridle, and it was Curtis. What was he doing here? He must have ran after me but why? Then he reached out his hand to me. I looked up at him into his eyes, I was hesitant but I wanted to trust him so I took his hand and he pulled me over the horse and I sat behind him. He motioned the horse to run, and when we reached the main gate, the Protectors saw that it was a Lord riding, so they opened the gate and let us passed through. We were outside the manor in the dark, and the horse kept running faster and faster. I didn't know where he was taking me but I didn't care. I placed my arm around his waist tightly and leaned against his back as the horse picked up more speed. I could only hear the horse's breathing and the sound of its powerful hooves each time it touches the ground in this still night. My tears started to dry as the cold strong wind blew on my face. We finally slowed down and I could hear flowing water nearby. We continued to ride until we reached and stopped near a riverbank. I went down from the horse first as Curtis offered his arm for support, and then he followed after. I stood there clutching my arms from the cold as I watched him hurriedly gathered some twigs nearby. He piled the woods and leaves and rubbed two stones together which after a while a fire came alive, and it grew bigger as he fed it more wood.

"You need to warm by the fire," he offered gently.

I was indeed cold so I did what he told me to do and sat near the fire trying to keep myself warm. Curtis took off his coat and placed it around my shoulders.

"Thank you," I said softly as I snuggled under it.

He sat not far from me and we stayed there not talking for a while. Was this my chance to escape? But I wondered why was he here, was he going to help me? It was very unlikely that he would do this and he had no reason to be here with me tonight. I didn't know what was he planning but I was tired of the awkward silence and so I faced him.

"Why are you doing this?" I softly asked.

"Doing what'" he gently asked confused staring at the fire.

"This. Why are you here?"

He paused before he gave an answer, "I couldn't just let you run away alone."

I was not expecting that answer from him. He was always so distant with me and so preoccupied with himself. Why would he suddenly say that?

"Honestly, I was hoping that you'd change your mind though," he added.

I was silent then resumed, "What if I don't?"

He didn't answer right away and it seemed that he was thinking, then he replied, "Then I have no choice but to come with you. I can't go back there alone, Andrew would kill me."

I didn't know how to respond to that. Was he serious?

He turned to face me, "But…. Running away isn't the answer. It's not going to solve anything and it would only make it worst," he explained.

I shook my head, "But I can't go back there, Andrew is…." My voice trailed off, it was hard talking about him.

"I know," he agreed quietly.

The fire continued to burn in the dark.

"Andrew would never change. He was always moody, manipulative, and obnoxious. So I do not blame you if you want to run away," he stated in a comforting tone, "I confess that there was a time that I wanted to leave too but I couldn't, partly because I didn't know where I would go," he threw a branch at the fire, "But…. if you need a reason to go back, you are not going back because of him. You are staying because you care for the people left behind. Without us, Andrew can do more damage and more people are going to get hurt. We cannot stop Andrew for sure but we can help those who had suffered by his hands."

I was speechless. It was the first time I heard of him speak of such words against Andrew and how much he seemed to genuinely care for Pinewood, and he was absolutely right. I hadn't thought of it that way. I was preoccupied on how miserable my life was living with Andrew that I hadn't consider those who had lived here around the longest under his rule. If I leave, it would not change anything.

"You're right. Things could get worst if I leave," I sadly agreed.

"And besides.... You're too popular to run away, everybody is going to notice you," he declared slightly grinning.

It was the first time I saw him smile and it was not at all disappointing.

"Popular?" I asked puzzled.

"Well, you made quite an impression to the villagers when you stood up for them at the First Village," he smiled some more.

"But I only said a few words," I spoke defensively.

"Apparently those few words made an impact and scared off the Captain. You're a hero to them now."

"What? I don't want to be a hero. You were there, you did more than I did," I objected.

"No," he shook his head while smiling, "they don't want me, they want you," he chuckled.

His laugh caught me off guard. I never saw him like this before, so at ease. I knew he was only trying to make me feel better and it was definitely working. His friendly disposition was a delightful surprise, and it made me wonder if this was what he really was inside all this time.

"You're serious aren't you?" I couldn't help but smile too, "Sorry but I don't have any intentions of becoming a hero."

He looked at me with warmth in his eyes, "All heroes never planned to be one, they are chosen by those who were inspired by them."

He spoke like he was not an Elite. He was the opposite of what I thought he was, and I felt like I was wrong about him. He was suddenly more friendly and I didn't know where this was coming from; it could be that he took pity of me after what Andrew said.

"I am sorry for tonight though," Curtis suddenly apologized.

"It's not your fault," I reassured solemnly.

"But still I could have said something."

"It's okay I didn't expect you to say anything at all in my defense."

He sighed, "It's just his way, he likes to provoke people, and if he sees you break, he would relish it and he won't stop."

"And he is good at it too, provoking people, that's why he enjoys it. I guess sometimes the only way not to give in to him is to stay silent," I sadly stated in disgust.

The night grew colder while I looked around beyond the trees behind us. It was so dark that anybody could be lurking in these woods. Curtis must had read my expression that he said, "Don't worry, I'll keep you safe."

I smiled at him which I never did before, it felt awkward at first but became natural after.

"But who was going to keep him safe?" I teased motioning my head towards the horse standing not far from us.

"Oh him?" he glanced at the horse, "No he's not going anywhere as long as I have his favorite treats right here in my pocket," he gleamed patting the right pocket on his pants.

There it was again, his smile. I was not aware then but when he smiles, it made him glow and strikingly more handsome. I couldn't help but see him differently tonight; I suddenly took noticed of everything about him.

The features on his face, his chiseled jawline, his piercing eyes that showed a hint of blue when the fire reflects on them, his gestures and his sudden gentle expression. They all seemed to resonate who he was and that made him very attractive.

"You were an animal doctor back then?" he spoke, suddenly interrupting my thoughts. His question was new to me, it was at a personal level but I didn't mind. It was a comforting change talking to someone about it.

I nodded, "Yes, it was something that I was always passionate about."

"It shows and you're really good at it like what you did with Mr. Conolly's horse."

"Oh, any animal doctor could do that," I spoke embarrassed by his praises.

"Well…. you're the only animal doctor I know; still it was impressive what you did."

"I guess…." I conceded reluctantly.

Curtis threw another branch at the fire and it continued to burn brightly, "It must have been terrible leaving home so suddenly," he spoke with a change of topic.

"It was. I thought my life would be over. I kept hoping that this was all a mistake…." My words faded as I spoke. I wondered if he thought that this was a mistake as well. It felt like he could be trusted but I was not sure if he felt the same way as I did about this.

"Someday you'll go back home," he said with assurance that I was hoping was true.

"I hope so," I prayed.

"Could you tell me more about your home?," he spoke softly.

I told him what it was like back home, the weather, what type of people lived there and what my typical day was at work. I didn't realize that I was smiling when I was talking about it; it made me happy, and homesick at the same time but I didn't mentioned to him about the man from across the street because it was a part of my life that I wasn't ever going to talk about to anyone. That life was long gone and soon would be forgotten.

CHAPTER 8: WILD HORSES

CURTIS

I was relieved when Elaine decided to return to the manor last night. I thought she was going to run away for good after what happened with Andrew. That night at the dining room was painful to watch. Andrew was out of control and what he said to her was truly unforgivable. One thing that surprised me though was when I ran after Elaine, I didn't know what exactly happened but a voice in my head told me to go after her and so I did without any second thoughts. I wanted to call out to her to stop but I knew she would not listen so instead I ran away with her, and it was invigorating just the two of us. I didn't know what came over me that night at the river; it was confusing at first but the more we talked, the more I couldn't resist looking at her. I was afraid that she might catch me staring as I tried to be inconspicuous. The way she was beaming with happiness when she talked about her home entranced me, and the sound of her voice I wanted to hear more of. There must have been something in the air that night that made it different yet special. I was thinking often of her as I walked aimlessly in the hallway. I was about to pass the library when suddenly the door opened and to my delightful surprise it was Elaine. Her presence stunned me, and I suddenly became nervous around her but in a good way. She took noticed that I was there probably standing like a fool, and before any of us could speak, I heard a little girl's voice shouting, "Ellie!"

We both turned and I saw Katrina was skipping towards us.

"I'm sorry I shouldn't have yelled that name, I forgot Curtis was here," Kat worriedly apologized.

"Huh?" I was confused.

"It's okay. I don't think he's going to tell anyone," Elaine warmly assured Kat.

"What's this all about?" I asked still puzzled.

Kat grinned, "She likes to be called Ellie."

"It's just something they call me back home," she tried to explain dismissively.

"Oh! Then we should call you Ellie then," I cheerfully suggested.

Elaine just gave an awkward smile then glanced at Kat, "So where are you off to?"

"I have a class in the library today," she replied sweetly.

"That's great! Come in then," Ellie directed her to the door and opened it for her, and just as Kat left, a voice called out my name.

"Lord Curtis."

I glanced at the hallway and it was Mr. Logan bounding towards my direction. Ellie was still at the hallway closing the library door glancing at his direction as well.

"Lord Curtis, His Grace would like to know if there are any new developments," Mr. Logan inquired.

"None at the moment, but I have been working with the Protectors as he ordered."

"His Grace will not be happy to hear that."

"Tell him I have been closely monitoring the villages and if he could leave me for once to do my job then maybe we would catch the Defiers sooner than later," I exclaimed annoyed by his lack in faith in me.

"Very well my Lord, His Grace is expecting you to be true to your word when you told him you will help him put an end to this rebellion."

"I am Lord of Pinewood, I will do my duty," I declared firmly.

Mr. Logan nodded and bowed then he took his leave. I was about to face Ellie when she suddenly blurted in a hushed voice, "You're helping Andrew?! And you're working with the Protectors now?! Why?" she gave me a look that I betrayed her and her disappointment only grieved me knowing that she felt this way.

"I am just doing my duty," I stammered, and it was all I could answer.

"You know how Andrew feels about the villagers," she reminded and I could hear the anger in her voice as she glared, "And I thought after last night you were different," and with that she stormed away from me while I stood there in agony by the pain that I caused her.

Days turned to weeks since Ellie hadn't spoken to me. I knew she was mad, and I wanted to explain to her but time was never on my favor, and each time she found out that I would leave for the villages with the Protectors, I saw it angered her more and then she would ignore me completely. Andrew was pleased when we intercepted a plan of attack from the Defiers. Explosives were found in an abandoned barn and it was to be used on another truck from the Steel Plants but no Defier were ever caught though. He was extremely satisfied with what I uncovered that my days were easier whenever I was around him.

It was late at night when I was in my private chambers. I was getting ready for a change in clothes when I heard a soft knock. Who could it be at this hour? I went to the door and slowly opened it, and I was surprised to see that it was Ellie who pushed it open and came directly inside without asking for my consent, and all the while ignoring me. It was all over her face that she was outraged and frustrated, her hair was down, and her dress was unbuttoned on the neck and the sleeves. I closed the door wondering what she was doing here.

"What were you thinking Curtis? I thought you were on my side not Andrew's," she was clearly disturbed and disgusted by what I did, and the look that she was betrayed was troubling me most but I was more taken aback when she finally said my name for the first time.

"I thought you hated him?" she continued with the same appalled expression.

I was searching for the right words then I explained, "What do you want me to do? You know the Defiers needs to be stopped."

"Yes but by helping Andrew? What you said that night at the river was it all true? Or did you just say it because you felt sorry for me?" she said her voice full of disappointment.

"I have no other choice...." I tried to explain.

"You're just saying that to hide the fact that you're actually a coward," she interrupted fuming.

Her words pierced through me, and I despised her accusing me of such but I took control and calmed myself down. Her words hurt me more than it angered me. I sighed feeling defeated, there was definitely no stopping her.

"I should have told you but I didn't want you to get involved," I spoke feeling gloomy, "I know there would be certain danger if you knew what I am about to tell you but I feel that you won't stop being persistent and you won't ever forgive me for what I did."

I paused, thinking if what I was about to say was wise

as she stood there patiently waiting. This could change our lives and whatever the outcome, I was willing to accept it if she wanted the answers. I stared at her gathering the strength I needed to say it.

"I am a Defier."

Ellie gasped and I saw her face turned from confused to shock. She slowly went to a nearby couch and sat there and I followed and sat beside her. I waited for her to recover which she finally did and looked at me in fear.

"Why would you help the rebels?" she silently asked.

I told her what Olfren said to me at Greendale Forest. How Andrew were enslaving innocent villagers to work at the Steel Plants. She listened silently and I could tell that she was finding it hard to believe as I did.

"The Defiers needed my help especially now that the Protectors are here," I explained.

"But.... I overheard you and Mr. Logan.... And the abandoned barn...." her voice trailed off as she sounded confuse.

I shook my head, "It was all pretend, staged with the help of the Defiers so that I would gain Andrew's trust completely and he would give me access to where he did not gave me before. We needed to be one step ahead of the Protectors and Andrew."

She remained silent staring down at the floor. This must had been too much for her that I regret saying what I said. I moved closer to her, "Ellie look at me," I gently asked, and she did, and I looked directly at her eyes and told her with my words full of sympathy, "I am sorry if I did this to you but sometimes I forget that my life is not my own anymore since we've been matched. I had no right to put your own life in danger because I became a Defier but if you tell me to end this right now, I would leave the Defiers for your sake."

I continued to gaze at her, and I thought I was going to find relief but instead I saw pity.

"I am not going to tell you to stop on one condition," she said softly but with determination, "that you let me join you."

"No you can't, I can't put you in danger" I said shaking my head, I was not expecting this and I was not very enthusiastic of the idea.

"But you already have by telling me, and by being one. I am your mate and the Empire would probably hold me accountable too for your actions if ever we were found out," she explained with insistence.

"This was a bad idea," I said it out loud full of remorse.

"You already got me involved so you might as well agree," she declared feeling so sure of herself.

"There's no stopping you is there?" I sighed, "Alright but you must always follow my lead," I firmly instructed.

"Deal," she willingly agreed.

"Good! In the meantime, we act normally to avoid suspicion," I suggested seriously.

"And normal is?"

I shrugged, "We don't talk to each other like we usually do especially around Andrew."

"Like we can't stand each other?"

"I guess."

"Well, that's not hard to do," she declared grinning.

"Wait…. What?"

She giggled, "I was only kidding," she sweetly teased.

This side of her, I didn't know that she was capable of it while being with me, and it was very refreshing, and I wanted more of her and seeing her happy was intoxicating.

"If we're going to work together, we might as well start getting to know each other," she explained as if she read my mind. We sat there in silence and I found myself gazing at her and it was hard letting go. She suddenly cleared her throat and I woke up from my trance that it got awkward after. She finally stood and hurriedly said, "It's getting late, I must return to my room, Good night." I stood up as well as she bounded for the door and left the room.

We were acting our usual selves as agreed since that night for the past few days. We were minding our own business but there would come a time when I wanted to see her, and I would look for excuses to run into her in the places where I knew she would be. One time I found her in the garden alone which was an opportunity for me to have a talk.

"I thought we agree to be inconspicuous?" she teased when she saw me approaching her.

I smiled, "Nobody ever comes out here."

We talked that day about her life back at Coastal City and about her parents. The way she talked about her home made me feel that I wanted to go there as well. She would sometimes asked about my own father and mother but I only dismissed the idea, and I saw on her face that it pained her when I refuse to talk about them.

"Maybe I could find a way for us to visit your home someday," I willingly offered.

It made her so enthusiastic, "Really could you do that?"

I smiled, "I could try but I must confess that it's going to be hard."

She became excited that she suddenly hugged me. I was startled but the way she held me, her sweet scent, and her closeness overpowered me.

She quickly released me realizing that what she did was just a spur of the moment, and she composed herself, smiling and said, "Inconspicuous."

My business with the Protectors continued. There would be a time that I would go with them to the villages. They still use force when searching and interrogating but I was there to make sure no one got hurt badly. Sometimes Captain Furlong would join and we act around each other like nothing happened before but it didn't mean I had respect for him, I only needed to be here and be the eyes and ears for the Defiers. Protectors heavily patrolled the villages and towns ever since the explosives were found in the abandoned barn, but it was necessary despite that it meant more guards and patrols. I was at the First Village making sure the Protectors did their job. It was then that I saw a villager stare at me in disgust. He probably thought I was helping the Protectors, I was not mad at him though, I only felt pity. If he only knew that I was here for them. I was approaching Mr. Conolly's house and two Protectors stood guard at his front yard. The village especially this house had lost its warmth and welcoming aura since the Protectors arrived. I went around to the barn and I was searching inside the stable and sure enough Mr. Conolly was there raking the hays.

"Mr. Conolly," I called from behind him almost in a whisper.

Mr. Conolly turned around and was not surprised that he saw me. He wiped the sweat on his brows with his hand and silently motioned me with his head to follow him. We went further inside the barn and stayed in a corner where stacks of hay hid us.

"My Lord, this is too dangerous," he warned in a hushed

voice his face still flushed red from his work.

"This was my only chance. So are we all set?" I inquired whispering.

He didn't answer but I saw the apprehension on his face.

"What's the matter?" I asked sounding worried.

"It would be quite hard or even impossible my Lord now that the Protectors have doubled the guards," he hesitantly explained.

"I'll deal with it. That's what I am here for. Tell the Defiers to push through, let me handle the rest," I assured him with firm confidence.

He only nodded.

"Good! Take care my friend," I said sincerely.

"Thank you my Lord."

We dispersed to our separate ways making sure no one saw us as I returned to the midst of the Protectors.

CHAPTER 9: THE GAME

ELAINE

It has been confusing for the past couple of days. Curtis had been friendly of late and I had no idea what changed him but I didn't mind it though, it felt uncomfortable at first but then having a friend was never a bad thing especially when I needed someone to talk to. I admit I was starting to enjoy his company and he made me happy sometimes, but I was ecstatic when he said he would try to find a way for us to visit home. That would be a day I would be looking forward to, and it was then when I decided that Curtis was actually a good man. When he told me he was a Defier, it was the farthest thing from my mind that I thought he would say. An Elite a Defier? Nothing like that had ever happened, not even in the history books. It was immensely impressive and the thought of it was overwhelming, and it had to be Curtis. He being a Defier spoke so much about his character, he had all the comfort and luxury and yet he risked everything. All his life he was living in the shadows of Andrew and his estranged father, then he finally stood up for himself and I wanted nothing more but to join him because the idea of creating change for the greater good was exhilarating.

I was staying alone in the Parlour one day enjoying my afternoon tea and biscuits placed on the coffee table in front of where I sat while watching out the window staring at the sky and the trees. Then Curtis suddenly appeared, I noticed lately our paths would meet more often than before but I welcomed his company. He was smiling when he approached and I smiled in return. He took a seat beside me as we shared the couch and a footman served him his tea. We sat there silently for a while admiring the view from outside when he spoke out of nowhere.

"So Ellie...." he began to say but stopped midsentence suddenly looking concerned, "Can I call you Ellie?" he stammered unsure of himself.

I giggled, "Yes you may."

There was relief on his face, "How was your day?"

I shrugged, "Nothing special."

He was grinning, "You seem bored. There must be something you want to do," he paused, "How about something you were curious to try when you were a Beta but couldn't?"

I was beaming and thinking then I finally said, "Well, I always wanted to try chocolates. I never tried them before. Where I came from, some people would give anything for a taste."

Curtis chuckled, "You never had chocolates?" he said in disbelief.

"Ummm.. No. Chocolate is a luxury we couldn't afford back home."

His smile broadened, "Then we shall have all kinds of chocolates delivered to your chambers every night," he declared merrily.

"Oh no that'll be too much and too expensive," I stated.

"Nonsense! Do you see all the useless valuable arts we have around here in the manor? I don't think spending on chocolates would matter much," he jested and laughed.

I laughed with him, and Curtis waved at a footman who was standing silently nearby and he hurriedly approached us.

"Please have someone deliver all kinds of chocolates to the Lady's chamber," he ordered grinning.

"Yes my Lord," the footman obliged, bowed then left the Parlour.

As soon as our laughter died down, we both reached at the same time for a biscuit when our hands accidently brushed against each other. The moment we touched I could feel myself suddenly becoming alive, like a bolt of lightning was running through me. We stayed like that for a while staring at each other. I felt myself blushing and was confused of what was happening but I didn't want to take my hand away just yet. Then I felt nervous and pulled my hand away quickly when I realized the footman was returning. We sat there silent like nothing had happened while we tried our best to hide our look of bewilderment and delight. The footman stood in front of Curtis unaware of what happened.

"My Lord, a letter for you," the footman formally presented it to Curtis which he accepted, and then he bowed then stood at the corner.

Curtis opened it, the envelope had two contents, an elegant looking card of dark gray color that glittered and shone, and a small note. I saw a seal and it was a head of a Ram at the back of the card when Curtis read it at the other side. His face lit up as his eyes scanned through the words then after that he read the small white note that came with it. He finally looked at me elated by what he just read.

"What is it?" I curiously inquired.

He briefly laughed, "Ambrose had been matched, and we're invited to the ceremony" he excitedly announced.

My face dropped when I heard what he said. It was not because Ambrose was matched but because it meant I had to go to another ceremony then a banquet would follow which I never had the desire to relive that agonizing event full of Elites.

"And guess what?" Curtis continued excitedly holding the small note up, "The Crowned Prince would be there."

I groaned, the Crowned Prince was heir to the throne and a Sovereign. If the Prince was going to attend then the banquet was going to be extremely extravagant and more superficial Elites were going to be there.

"What's the matter?" Curtis face became worried when he noticed my expression.

"I can't go to another banquet, it was hard for me then and it's going to be harder for me in such a larger setting" I anxiously objected.

"Don't worry. I'll be there with you this time," he tenderly assured me.

"But we will be the laughing stock of everybody. This has more intimidating people, and I was not made to attend such lavish party at this magnitude," I explained further worried of our fate.

Curtis sat there without saying a word. I hope he understood what I meant and that I didn't ever want to go. I was uncomfortable with his silence until he finally spoke.

"I have a plan," he calmly declared, "I know the Elites are going to be talking about us at the banquet especially about you. Yes they will test and intimidate you, asking you questions or fishing for your opinion until they will find a flaw in you."

His words were not helping or comforting me at all and it only aggravated my fears.

"But...." he continued, "instead of cowering and fearing to be judged, let them judge you then, but you're going to impress them. Catch them off guard, they won't be expecting it."

"Impress how?" I asked confused.

"With everything you already are. Your charm, your beauty, your strength, and the advantage that you are different from them. You were Beta that rose to the ranks of the Elites," he explained confidently.

"I don't know. How can I be charming when I'm panicking? And you know very well I am never charming especially around Elites," I declared feeling hopeless.

He smiled, "Don't underestimate yourself Ellie. Just play their game and they will adore you."

I sighed defeated, "I don't have a choice do I?

"You can do this Ellie. I won't leave your side."

"I don't even know what to wear," I said feeling depressed.

"Not to worry, Miss Pattilyn would take care of it," he assured cheerfully.

There was no way out of this so I guess I had to play the part. This was going to be a game for the Elites of predator and prey, and I was pretty sure I was the prey.

I was at the stables brushing the horses. Mr. Witherson was not happy that I was there at all as he kept on complaining that a Lady should never brush a horse and that it was his job. I only laughed at his gloomy disposition and teased him that I was no Lady and that I was more than happy to help him. While I was brushing a brown mare, Miss Pattilyn came.

"AAhhh... My Lady, glad that I finally found you! You have an appointment today with Mrs. Rouge."

"Mrs. Rogue?" I asked while brushing.

"Yes my Lady, a fashion designer one of the best. Lord Curtis instructed me to call her and have her come to have you fitted for your banquet gown," she declared excitedly. I almost forgot about the gown, the thought of the coming banquet made my stomach squeeze.

I followed Miss Pattilyn to the drawing room and when I entered, an attractive very high fashion slender woman with short blonde hair and she looked like she was in her forties greeted us with a huge smile.

"My Lady," she curtsied then gracefully took my hand and held it, "It's an honor to have finally met you, I have heard so much about you," she said in a sultry voice with a hint of foreign accent and she was genuinely smiling but all the while subtly examining me from head to toe, and there was a brief disappointed look on her face when she realized that I was only wearing beige riding pants, white shirt, and black riding boots, improper for a Lady when receiving guests but she kept on smiling after nonetheless.

"Shall we begin?" she happily asked.

Two of her assistants, one male the other female, ushered me in front of a full body mirror that they set up. The female assistant took my measurements while the male wrote it down. Meanwhile Mrs. Rouge was studying my figure, and talking about the right kind of design and color and the fabric to use that would suit me. I didn't understand what she was saying though since fashion was never my forte so I just smiled each time she said something to me. After they took my measurements, the assistants opened a large black metal suitcase where they took out rolls of very fine fabrics of different colors, and placed one and sometimes two against my body while Mrs. Rogue watched while deciding which was the best.

"Hmmm... not that one June, maybe the other one,"

she suggested crossing her arms.

The female assistant returned the fabric she was holding then took another, this time it was of a certain shade of blue and placed it against me.

"Perfect! Don't you agree," Mrs. Rogue looked at me waiting for my confirmation.

"It's beautiful," I agreed as I felt the fabric so soft, light, and cool and the shade was beyond elegant.

"The color looks stunning on you my Lady," Miss Pattilyn complimented.

"I agree," Mrs. Rogue nodded contented, "Francis," she was referring to her male assistant who approached and held my hair up gently as she studied my face.

"She would look absolutely gorgeous with her hair up and make up on," Mrs. Rogue stated to Francis as she continued to stare and study my face.

"Well! I think we're done here," she declared and gave two continuous brief claps.

June and Francis then packed everything back to the large suitcase and folded the mirror, and while they were packing, Mrs. Rogue stood closer in front of me and gazed smiling, "Oh my dear, I am sure she would have been so proud of you if she was here," she said softly and sincerely as I could smell her sweet flowery scent.

"I am sorry but who do you mean?" I politely asked.

"Why Lady Loren of course. She was a good friend of mine and I made all of her banquet gowns," she gently answered, "and soon you'll be wearing one of mine, and with it you will represent change."

CHAPTER 10: BLACKARD

CURTIS

 Ambrose's wedding was today, and I couldn't help but feel happy for him that he was matched and I hoped that he agreed with his mate. I was looking forward to seeing him again but I was anxious for the banquet. I shared Ellie's nervousness and I was not going to tell her that when she needed my help the most, but I believe in her though. I was the first one to arrive at the manor's shuttle dock. As I waited outside a silver shuttle's entrance, I observed that the household was busy today as they prepared for our departure. Footmen were placing our luggage on the shuttle that would take us to Blackard, and Mr. Thistle was giving the orders to everyone trying to keep them on schedule. Then Ellie arrived shortly after, wearing a lavender and white long sleeved dress looking more stunning than the flower itself. Mrs. Pattilyn followed behind her carrying some of her personal bags. Ellie stopped in front of me while Miss Pattilyn proceeded to enter the shuttle. I gave her my warmest smile and I could tell that she was nervous today.

"Are you okay?" I tilted my head.

She sighed, "Is there any way I could cancel this trip?"

I chuckled, "It'll be fine. Just enjoy this. Have you ever been to Blackard?"

"I've never been there," she replied shaking her head.

"So have I. I guess this would be an adventure then. Isn't it exciting?" I declared enthusiastically.

She finally smiled, "I am a bit excited to go there," she admitted.

"I'm sure we're going to love it there, I heard it was a

beautiful place."

"Are you trying to cheer me up?" Ellie teased grinning.

"Maybe… is it working?" I teased back.

She let out a small laugh and I could feel myself melting for her.

Andrew arrived with Katherine beside him and Mr. Logan followed behind. Our mood changed when we saw Andrew. Ellie was glaring at him and I watched as they approach the shuttle entrance.

Andrew sneered and mockingly said, "Little brother, you and your little bird there are going to be the entertainment at the banquet." He laughed as they entered the shuttle.

"Ignore him," I suggested to Ellie who didn't say anything.

We entered the shuttle shortly after. Some of the members of the household accompanied us including Miss Pattilyn and Mr. Thistle who took their seats in a different chamber. Ellie and I took the couch seat facing each other with a circular table in between us at the far corner of the shuttle away as much as possible from Andrew. I knew he was invited as well, so were the rest of the wealthy and powerful Elites in the Empire, but I was not going to let him spoil this trip for us. We stayed in one area in the Elite's chamber in the shuttle. Our chamber was more like an elegant living room with expensive carpets, large couches, and wooden tables, and large glass windows that you could almost see everything outside. The shuttle started to ascend bound for Blackard. Ellie was looking outside the window as we flew and while she had not notice, I couldn't resist admiring her long lashes, flawless skin, her perfect elegant jawline and red lips, and those amazing green eyes that sparkled as the light of the sun touched his face, and I would quickly pretend to look down whenever she would try to glance at my direction. Mr. Thistle and some Footmen came in to serve us different varieties of Hors D'oeuvres on round trays each type more colorful and elegant and wine was served in clear stylish glasses. Ellie was delighted when she saw what they were serving that she had difficulty choosing.

"We should make a toast," I happily declared while holding my glass.

Her eyes were beaming as she glanced at me smiling, "To what?"

"Hmmm… How about to us? Whatever happens at the banquet, we stick together," I willingly suggested.

"I like that," she agreed.

"To us," I raised my glass towards her.

"To us," she repeated and did the same then we drank our wine.

We continued to sit comfortably on our chairs and soon Ellie fell asleep. She looked so serene while napping that I was careful not to wake her up. I looked around the shuttle and I saw Andrew and Mr. Logan deep in conversation. I wonder what they were talking about. Although Andrew trusted me, he was always careful not to involved me too much in his business affairs maybe in fear that I might find out what he had been doing in the Steel Plants. I had my ways though to know what he was planning, his office was not always inaccessible and I just need to be careful not to get caught or everything would be over.

A couple of hours have passed. I gazed down outside the window and it was cloudy at first but after a few moments, it departed revealing nothing but white on the ground. We finally arrived at Blackard.

"Ellie," I softly woke her up, "Ellie," I gently repeated.

She finally stirred on her seat and slowly opened her eyes.

"We're here," I cheerfully said nodding towards the glass window.

She sat up straight then looked out, "Snow," she gasped in amazement.

"Yes, it's winter in Blackard right now," I confirmed.

"It's beautiful," she admired, "I've never seen snow before," she added.

"Blackard is always cold all year round that sometimes it would snow even during their summer," I stated.

The shuttle started to descend and by this time we were flying over a large city covered in snow. It was a cloudy day but from time to time the sun would shine through the clouds and its rays would make the snow glitter like diamonds all over the city. We landed on a shuttle dock and the footmen assisted us with our fur cloaks to keep us warm. Andrew exited the shuttle first followed by Katherine, Mr. Logan, and Mr. Thistle and rode in a large luxury vehicle and drove off while we took the next one with Miss Pattilyn.

We were on our way, the snow stopped falling and the streets of Blackard were cleared of it, a variety of magnificent slick dark gray sky scrapers that reached the clouds stood out among the smaller buildings that you could hardly see the top when you were looking down from a car window, and the people in the city all wore heavy thick coats or cloaks but despite the very cold weather, they seemed to be used to it.

"Where are we headed?" Ellie asked.

"My family has a house here so we'll be staying there," I responded.

"Another house with Andrew?" she expressed wryly.

"It's a large house, not as big as the manor back home but I don't think we would run into him inside."

We arrived at our destination and a Footman opened the door for us when we stopped on the driveway. The house was still located in the city, in an enclosed neighborhood with the other large houses owned by Elites. It had a more simple architectural design, homier atmosphere but just as elegant compared to the manor. Andrew was already inside and Mr. Thistle greeted us at the door and took our cloaks while he told a Footman to take us to our room. Inside the house, the walls and the shiny floors were of light beige and so was the wide staircase that ascended to our rooms. The footman opened a mahogany colored double door which he announced was our room, and I saw the terrified look on Ellie's face when I glanced at her direction.

"You can have this room, I'll take the one beside it," I offered to her.

"Thank you," Ellie said with a hint of relief.

Moments after, I heard a gentle knock on my door and when I opened it, I found Ellie standing in her long black fur boots, white pants with a black buckle, and black knitted top that covered her neck which she wore under a white thick fur coat with black buttons and a hood, and black leather gloves. She always looked so good no matter what she wore even if it was not a Lady's clothes but she always did what she pleases.

"Aren't you coming?" she asked excitedly.

I assumed we were going out, "Let me grab my coat first," I chuckled.

Miss Pattilyn hurried over our direction before we left the house.

"My Lady, my Lord, please be reminded to be back

at four this afternoon, my Lady's gown will arrived by then," she requested.

"We'll be back before then Miss Pattilyn," I promised.

We started off walking around the neighborhood admiring the houses then it wasn't long when we reached the shops. Ellie was excited gazing at almost anything as we reached the display windows. There were bakeries, souvenir shops, clothes shops, ornaments and many more in this busy district. She had fun passing by them and sometimes we would enter the store if something caught her eye and I didn't mind though; her company was enough to make me happy. We were fascinated about everything in Blackard. We even tried the warm food and hot drinks that they sold beside the streets which seemed to be popular and it helped a lot especially when the weather grew colder as the day was getting late. We touched the snow that was on the sidewalk with our bare hand and was amused by its texture.

"I think I like snow," Ellie declared delighted while I laughed at her comment, she looked genuinely delighted to have seen snow, and her laughter and smiles that she wore the whole time was invigorating.

We eventually got back to the house and Miss Pattilyn was extremely disappointed when we arrived late that she foresees us missing the ceremony. I repeatedly apologized to her but we had so much fun exploring the city that we lost track of the time. Mrs. Rouge's assistants, June and Francis, were already there and took Ellie to her room for the preparations.

I was wearing a fine dark blue tail coat, it had diamond buttons that ran at the center, and elegant curves embroidered on my chest down to the waist studded with little diamond stones all over, and a white soft formal shirt under a white vest, and white pants with black buckles, and long black shiny leather boots. Mrs. Rouge had outdone herself this time I thought. I knocked at Ellie's door when it was almost time to go. Miss Pattilyn opened and ushered me through. There she was in the middle of the room, standing like a magnificent creature. She was shining brilliantly in her long wide gown of a different shade of blue like cobalt that splendidly exposed her shoulders, chest, and back. Layers of diamonds that elegantly curved and spiraled on her waist and on the edges of her skirt. She wore a diamond necklace that glittered on her skin and diamond earrings that dangled, and shines when they sway. Her hair was neatly held up by a diamond band that was shaped like a serpentine. She was breathtaking and I thought nobody was as glamorous as her tonight. She had bewitched me and that was when I knew that I had completely fallen for her. Ellie smiled when she saw me, "What do you think?" she asked while turning around.

I shook my head beaming at her, "You are going to outshine everybody tonight."

We missed the ceremony so we rode the car on the way to the banquet and Ellie was not at all disappointed but I could see how nervous she was when she rubbed her palm with her fingers and so I was thinking of ways to calm her down.

"Did you know that Blackard's sigil is a ram?" I suddenly said in a comforting manner.

She didn't say anything as she continued to nervously fidget.

"Blackard has plenty of sheep but the ram is special that they would never kill them," I informed, "Although,

I heard somewhere that they were special because of their, you know..... dung," I added smiling.

"What?" she asked bewildered as I finally caught her attention.

"Their dung is like gold here in Blackard. They believed that the ram's dung that drops on the ground turns to oil that's why Blackard is rich," I explained grinning.

Her puzzled look turned to laughter, "That's the silliest thing I have ever heard."

I laughed with her shaking my head, "It is, isn't?"

The car rang with our laughter but when it died down, there were more nervous silence. I gently placed my hand over hers, and the sudden motion startled her but she didn't take her hand away, then I looked at her and assured softly, "Everything is going to be alright Ellie, you can do this." She smiled warmly and took a deep breath. Our car slowed down on the large driveway of the House of Craye. Cars waited in line for their turn as more Elites poured out the large driveway entering the manor. When it was our time, a footman opened the car door and I exited first then offered my hand to Ellie and she held it when she got off from the car. Snow was lazily falling tonight when we made our way to the entrance. Ellie was admiring the marvelous manor of the Craye's that was as huge as ours back in Pinewood. Inside the manor the walls were black with white elegant wall moldings, and the floors were black as well with white exquisite carpets and the large tall windows were draped in white curtains with stylish light gray designs. Ellie had her hand around my arm when we made our way to the banquet hall where footmen in black formal stood at attention along the corridors. Art paintings of different styles where hung but we didn't stop to admire them. We were approaching a large entrance with large white graceful arches above it then I stopped before proceeding and glanced at Ellie smiling, "Are you ready?" She nervously nodded.

"Don't forget to smile," I reminded grinning.

We entered the grand banquet hall, it had a wide white staircase, and at first, it looked like the hall was open air with exits framed in large white arches with no doors and it leads out to the large balcony into the cold black snowy night but if you look closely, the balcony were actually completely covered in glass shields on the outside that it was so clear you would not notice it and it prevented the snow from falling on the open balcony. We slowly descended the wide stairs together with some Elites who arrived with us, and sure enough some of the guests in their expensive gowns and suits, one trying to outshine the other, who were already there took notice of our entrance. Some stared while others gazed in awe, then some gawked at her, some started to whisper, and others subtly pointed their fingers at us while talking. Ellie suddenly tightened her grip on my arm as we reached the bottom steps and made our way through the crowd. I realized that they were mostly staring at Ellie, and I could feel that even when we passed they continued staring behind our backs. I was proud of her that night the way she handled herself with such elegance and style constantly smiling that you would forget that she was not born an Elite. '*Yes she is here and she demands your undivided attention,*' it was what I told myself when I glanced and was amused by the Elites and their reactions. The orchestra above us that was playing classical music paused then resumed with a different tune after a footman announced the arrival of the Craye family. The attention of the Elites shifted then to the entrance above the stairs. The members of the House of Craye and their new addition all entered looking ravishing in their fine clothes. Ambrose looked especially happy which was a good sign. Some guest flocked in their direction to offer their compliments to the family and the newly matched. Soon after, the food was served in bite sizes and we took some and drank our wine as we stood away from the crowd when a familiar figure was approaching us.

"Nigel!" I called out cheerfully.

"Curtis!" he waved grinning.

We shook hands firmly when he arrived where we were standing.

"'It's good to see you again," I declared smiling.

"Same to you my friend. I only regret that I missed your own ceremony."

"Don't worry about it," I assured dismissively, "Let me introduce to you my mate Lady Elaine," I continued.

Nigel gallantly bowed and smiled then Ellie curtsied in return.

"It's my pleasure to meet you my Lady," he shyly greeted.

Ellie smiled widely, "Same to you my Lord."

Nigel nervously stood still grinning without saying a word.

I chuckled, "Please forgive my friend here but he is extremely shy with large group of Elites especially around a Lady," I explained to Ellie.

Ellie giggled, "I feel exactly the same way my Lord. At best, two or three Elites I could tolerate."

I saw Nigel's mood relaxed when he laughed at Ellie's comment. They continued to have a friendly chat when I noticed a couple of Elites nearby staring at our direction, and then started to slowly approach me. I knew their names from previous friendly acquaintances; he was Lord Jesse Prime, a strong man who was in his early thirties and his mate Lady Mira, a pleasant looking slender woman with all smiles and was a few years older than him.

"Lord Curtis, I don't know if you remember me?" Lord Jesse greeted grinning.

"I do remember you Lord Jesse," I politely respond.

He smiled then continued, "It's good to see you, I hope life treats you well."

"As well as can be expected."

"That's wonderful my Lord, and your mate?" Lord Jesse inquired glancing at Ellie, and by that I understood his hint that he wanted to be introduced. I didn't see the harm in that so I motioned them closer to Ellie who was conversing with Nigel.

"I'm sorry to interrupt. Lady Elaine may I present to you Lord Jesse and Lady Mira," I introduced them to her.

Ellie smiled then elegantly curtsied to them, and in return Lady Mira did the same while Lord Jesse bowed. I was impressed by how Ellie presented herself; her previous lessons must had been of great help. Lady Mira immediately became friendly with Ellie and soon Lord Jesse, and they talked about how they heard so much about her and wanted to meet her in person. I couldn't help but smile as I stood there not far, observing while they started conversing among themselves and they enjoyed her company and were fascinated by her. Soon after, more joined their group, those who were curious and captivated by her and she continued to treat them with dignity and grace; yet some who were nearby continued to look on with disgust.

The orchestra suddenly stopped playing and the sound of heavy marching could be heard approaching the hall. A footman who was at the entrance formally announced, "His royal highness, the Crowned Prince." Everybody in the hall stopped what they were doing and shifted their gaze to the entrance. The royal guards in their black and red uniform continued to march in two lines then descended on each side of the stairs and they stopped as the first guard who entered reached the last bottom steps, and then stood at attention then faced in unison towards the center of the staircase as the Crowned Prince entered then walked down the middle. The Prince wore a magnificent dark green tailcoat and pants with elegant prints of a darker shade made from the most expensive fabric and with white undershirt underneath a gold vest, and a soft white scarf around his neck that glittered and was tucked under his undershirt, and his black long boots with gold laces on the sides. He had a long well-kept pale blonde hair and light blue eyes that were piercing on his slender face. He had a tall and lean built unlike his father the Emperor who was robust, and he moved in an elegant and gentle fashion and had a vain expression on his face. We all bowed and the Ladies all curtsied in silence.

"Well don't stop the party on my account," he declared with his soft voice in an irritated yet delicate manner when he reached the bottom steps.

The orchestra immediately resumed playing an up-tempo song. We were standing on the far side of the hall but I could see the members of the House of Craye greeted the Prince and other Elites nearby were anxiously waiting to a have a turn with the Prince, probably to introduce themselves and gain his favor. The little crowd around Ellie dispersed like startled ants after the arrival of the Prince and they made their way to his direction except for Lord Jesse and Lady Mira who remained nearby away from the commotion. The Prince continued to look bored and annoyed. I pity him though, being surrounded by the exquisite and excessive all the time that nothing impresses him anymore. We continued to be by ourselves, Ellie resumed her conversation with Nigel and I watched towards Ambrose's direction thinking when I would have the time to speak to him. The Prince continued to walk forward and talk to some of the Elites while ignoring others or walked away if they did not interest him. Then all of a sudden, his expression changed as if he caught sight of something that intrigued him. I didn't have a clue what suddenly made him change his direction but I noticed that he was then coming our way.

"Oh no," I muttered disheartened.

Ellie and Nigel heard me and were confused.

"What is it?" Ellie asked.

I nodded at the Prince's direction, "Don't look now but I think he is coming over here," I declared.

Ellie started to panic, "What am I going to do?" she whispered with a worried look.

"Just calm down and be yourself Ellie. He is no different from anybody else here, you can do this," I calmly said in a hushed voice.

It calmed Ellie and she subtly nodded in agreement but I could still see in her eyes that she was terrified. The Elites who watched the Prince were baffled when they noticed that he was coming towards our direction. I instinctively stayed close beside Ellie then I bowed and she curtsied when he finally came upon us.

"You're a pretty little thing," the Prince commented in his melodic voice and observing Ellie while completely ignoring me and the rest.

She continued to stand nervously not knowing how to react to him.

"What's your name?" he asked sounding uninterested.

"Lady Elaine your highness."

"Hmmm.... Lady Elaine...." he repeated slowly, "I haven't seen you around before, why is that?" showing a dramatic curiosity while he asked.

"Don't tell me!" he commanded quickly interrupting her before she could speak.

He paused and was thinking then he spoke, "You're the Beta turned Elite are you?"

"Yes your highness," Ellie politely answered.

"I must say....," he said softly and slowly contented that he got it right, then sneered and came closer to Ellie, too close that it made me uncomfortable, "You're a little flower sticking out from among these thorns, too delicate and beautiful, yet too out of place. It's best you return to where you came from little flower," he had a vain look and a mocking smile.

I felt uneasy then I glanced at Ellie, she didn't show any reaction but there was a sudden confidence in her eyes then she warmly smiled and said, "Thank you your highness, that's the greatest compliment anybody has given me since I became an Elite."

We all stood there in silence then the Prince suddenly laughed in a soft and pleasant way. I was stunned and so were the other Elites who were watching, I never saw him laugh that much before.

"I like you, you're feisty" the Prince declared cheerfully this time and was grinning, "Let's have a chat," he said while he ushered her farther away from where we stood while continuing to ignore everybody else, and she obliged with a broad smile. I was dumbfounded, what had just happened? That someone as vain as the Prince enjoyed Ellie's company, and he knew she was Beta. They continued to talk moments later, just the two of them but I can't hear what they were saying. Once in a while I would hear him softly laugh then sometimes Ellie would giggle. The longer they talked, the more it became unbearable that it made me feel something that I have never felt before…. I was jealous of him.

I was startled when someone suddenly placed a hand on my shoulder. I turned around then.

"Ambrose! Congratulations!" I greeted while beaming then we shook hands.

"Thank you Curtis. It is indeed a happy day for me."

"You should be, your mate is gorgeous."

Ambrose chuckled, "So how are you and Lady Elaine?"

"We're doing good," I answered.

"Well after tonight, I think Lady Elaine is going to be very popular," he glanced at Ellie and the Prince.

"I hope so because she really deserves their respect" I nodded and grinned.

Ambrose, Nigel and I continued to catch up until he was summoned by his father and had to leave. Then Nigel was approached by another Lord who was a friend to his father and asked about him. I stood there alone frequently glancing at Ellie until it was time for the Prince to say his goodbyes. He seemed delighted to be with her and was amused that he left the banquet more cheerful than when he arrived. As soon as the Prince left, others started to follow and the guests started to dwindle. I looked at Ellie smiling then she glanced and smiled in return. I silently motioned my head towards the balcony and she understood then nodded.

Ellie and I were alone outside fascinated by the surrounding shields and how it protected the hall from the cold. Snow was falling heavily tonight and everything was dark outside except for the white silhouette where the moonlight touches, and it reflected from the snow to the shields illuminating the balcony with a glow. The snow did not touch the shields as it fell freely while the two of us watched. Ellie slowly reached out her hand and gently touched the shield, and I could see her cold breath escaping then she smiled in amazement, and when she released, she stopped feeling the cold then. I turned to face her, the glow in the balcony made her look so divine that something took over me, and seeing her like this, at the brim of perfection of everything that she was, her beauty and even her faults made me powerless that I felt every being of me belonged to her.

"Ellie," I tenderly called out her name.

She turned to look at me and suddenly it was hard to speak, and I never felt so nervous before.

"You were impressive tonight," I said sweetly.

She smiled awkwardly then said, "Believe me there were times when I wanted to run away from here."

I shook my head, "But you're the bravest woman I know."

She didn't say a word then I hesitantly slowly started to get closer not taking my eyes off her, and I could see her breathing heavily. We were face to face that I could feel her warm breath. I desired to be near her, to be close, did she felt the same way as I did? I could sense that she was confused but I have never been so sure of what I wanted until this moment so I closed my eyes and slowly leaned forward and ever so lightly our lips touched reluctantly. I was in pure bliss when her sweet lips did not pull away from mine. I held her arm carefully, afraid that I might fall but it was too late, I had fallen so completely in love with her. She became my entire world and I was having great difficulty grasping the reality of this captivating moment and all the while hoping for the possibility of its eternity.

CHAPTER 11: IMPULSE

ELAINE

I was pleasantly alarmed when he came closer with those tender piercing blue eyes as we stood on the balcony. He was surprisingly affectionate and I did not know how to respond because I was unsure of my feelings towards him. Indeed he was kind to me but I was not ready to discover what lies beyond his kindness. I wanted to say something to stop this but I couldn't, maybe I was just fascinated of the thought of what it would be like to be desired by someone so dazzling like him. My heart was pounding fast, yet everything seemed to move so slowly. My chest was about to burst when I unconsciously closed my eyes and my lips softly touched his. Was this a right choice? I had my doubts but I could not refrain myself from being enraptured, and the feeling was so intoxicating so I completely surrendered myself to him and to the surrealness of all this. I slowly wrapped my arms around his neck and pulled him gently closer for a deeper kiss and he responded eagerly. My knees were about to falter as we let our lips silently tell each other's longing impulse. We parted eventually but remained close that I felt his warm breath and I didn't open my eyes right away as I was remarkably still overwhelmed.

We were on the shuttle the next day returning to Pinewood and that morning I woke up feeling surprisingly elated. Curtis and I continued to keep our distance while we flew with Andrew but Curtis was having a hard time maintaining a straight face the entire flight when he constantly smiled at me and stealing moments for a chance to touch my hand secretly. I was looking down at

Blackard when our shuttle departed. Snow still covered the ground but it made the place look so magical and I was going to miss this place, and I couldn't have been more relieved that the banquet was finally over. Talking with the Crowned Prince last night was very intimidating. I thought him to be respectable but he was like any other Elites in that hall except that he was vainer and more self-absorb but at least he was not pretentious, it was just who he was, and he knew what he wanted and how to get it and he was not shy about it at all. He loved talking about himself and his love for art, and he criticizes anything that displeases or does not interest him. I thought that his only reason for talking to me was his fascination of my predicament, a Beta turned Elite, but then I think he really wanted to talk to someone that was different from all of them. Despite all that, I was grateful that he chose to speak to me that night and I admit he was slightly amusing in his own way.

  Curtis and I spent our time that day at the Parlour after we had our dinner back in Pinewood. He was playing the grand piano which impressed me since I didn't know he played and he did it beautifully while I sat on the couch listening. He always would glance at me with such fondness and smile tenderly while he played, and I was not used to this new affections he had, I think maybe my feelings were not of the same degree as his but I liked the way he look at me though, I would simply melt, and sometimes I would yearn for his company, like tonight, just the two of us was enough without even the need for words. Our peaceful time together was suddenly interrupted by Andrew who entered the Parlour with Katherine following closely behind. He sat at the couch across from me and Katherine beside him. I felt myself frowning then Curtis stopped playing.

"What are you doing here?" Curtis said sounding annoyed.

"Can't I spend my time here also?" Andrew defensively asked, "Keep on playing," he ordered Curtis with a calm voice.

Curtis glared at him then resumed playing the piano. I wanted to leave that room, the mere presence of Andrew was dreadful like he obliterates any form of happiness and it pleases him so.

"So, how was your night with the Prince?" he asked in a surprisingly friendly approach while he looked at my direction.

I didn't know how to answer him and I didn't want to so I ignored him.

Andrew sighed, "Look, I just want to talk, I don't think there is anything wrong with that, right?" he said grinning.

I didn't know what he was up to, he had a different mood tonight, and it was an odd thing and I didn't trust him so I continued to ignore him.

"Fine! Do you want me to apologize? Then I'm sorry," Andrew declared halfheartedly while he comfortably leaned his back on the couch.

He was toying with me. What was he up to?

"What did you talked about with the Prince?" he persistently asked.

I glared at him then studied his face then finally answered briefly, "Art."

He smirked, "You were talking to the second most powerful man in the Empire and all you talked about was art?!"

I nodded confidently then I decided to play along with

his game, "He seemed to enjoy it though, and he even insisted that I go take a look with him if I had the chance," I declared proudly.

I saw Andrew's face dropped. There it was. Do you think I didn't know how to play the Elite's game?

"He said he has a manor where all his precious art collections were stored and that I can stay there as long as I pleased," I added snobbishly and I heard Curtis chuckled while he continued to play the piano.

Andrew clenched his teeth then smiled.

"Did he say you could bring more along with you?" he inquired reluctantly.

It was then when Curtis pressed the piano keys all at once then he laughed and stood up, and took a seat beside me.

"Face it Andrew, now is the time for you to be nice to Elaine," Curtis declared triumphantly.

Andrew laughed, "I don't know what you are talking about."

Curtis sneered, "You know what I mean. She has won the favor of the Prince while you remained outside the circle. When we will see him again, he will continue to ignore you while he will lavish her with all his attention just like what he did at the banquet," he said so sure of his words.

Andrew sat in silence but in a flash that startled all of us, he abruptly lunged across the table at Curtis, his face full of rage. I heard Katherine shouted his name but he was so out of it that he punched Curtis on the face and then they fell on the floor with the couch and the table in disarray. Andrew was hovering over Curtis firmly clutching his collar and was about to hit him again with his other fist but before he could do that I threw myself over

Curtis.

"Stop! Enough!" I shouted.

I thought Andrew was going to hit me as well but I didn't move away though, "You wouldn't hit a Lady would you?" I angrily demanded and glared straight at him unafraid.

Andrew finally relaxed his fists and I saw his face returned to its color while Katherine stood there not far from us frightened. He let go of Curtis then stood up and composed himself then left the Parlour without saying a word. Katherine stayed and helped me with Curtis on his feet then we placed him on the couch.

"I'm fine," he groaned clearly in pain.

"I'll go get help," Katherine offered.

"No.... I said I'm fine," Curtis insisted.

I looked at Katherine and assured her, "It's okay, I'll take care of him."

Katherine hesitated then nodded and left the Parlour. I knelt in front of Curtis examining the red and blue discoloration on his cheekbone, "That's going to darkened tomorrow," I stated concerned. I was surprised when Curtis started to softly chuckled then sighed and said, "I finally got to him didn't I?"

We both laughed triumphantly together. I smiled at him warmly as he gently held my hand that was on his face and he smiled back then placed a gentle kiss on my palm. It hurt me when I saw Curtis in pain that I wanted to protect him. I felt that I was the only one for him and he was the only one for me but I had my doubts if this was all even real, or was this something I only needed to ease my own pain for losing my past.

CHAPTER 12: CONSEQUENCES
CURTIS

Peter and I were on our horses riding for Greendale forest on a cloudy day. We arrived at the agreed spot and Olfren was already there waiting. We climbed down from our horses and I gave the reigns to Peter, and then I slowly approached Olfren.

"What's that on your face?" he inquired while squinting his eyes to examine the healing bruise from afar.

"It's nothing," I replied dismissively, "So where are we?"

He didn't ask any further, instead he looked at me with confidence and replied, "Everything is set. The plan would be successful if all goes well."

I nodded, "I hope it does, I did my part, now it's time to do yours."

"The information you relayed to us was very useful so no doubt the operation will run smoothly," he explained.

"Good! Soon then?"

"Yes," he nodded, "Any day now."

Then I gave him a skeptical look, "What happens after?"

Olfren gave a faint smile, "Hopefully change will come, and if it does, it's going to hit hard, and you and me my friend are at the front seat."

"Let's just keep it this way that none of them knows that I helped."

"Your secret is safe with us," he assured.

I studied his words hoping that he would keep it that way, "Goodbye then," I finally said breaking the silence but as I was about to go back to my horse, Olfren called out, "I don't know when we'll see each other again, so now might be the perfect time to tell you that it's time for you to meet Ryder."

"Who?" I asked.

"Our leader."

I was not too keen of the idea of meeting their leader because it was going to be too risky; getting caught would mean treason and death, but it was very tempting offer though.

"I am not so sure that would be wise," I responded uncertain.

"But you would want to meet Ryder to have all the answers to your questions, it's what you always wanted," he insisted.

I didn't say a word, and he must have noticed my hesitation then he came close for a whisper, "If you change your mind, go to Gelhem."

He gave me one last stare that told me that I was in too deep involved with the Defiers that I cannot refuse this. Olfren rode his own horse but before he left he said, "Besides, aren't you curious of the future?"

    Weeks have passed since I last saw Olfren. Any day he said but the anticipation was killing me. I was with Ellie though spending another beautiful day outside in the garden. The wind was cool and the sun was trying to escape from the clouds but to no avail. We were walking across the garden and new flowers of different colors and shapes have fully bloomed. Squirrels had taken up residence on a nearby tree were they played around hopping up and down on the branches, and a couple of swans flew towards the large pond not far from here. In the midst of all this, I embraced and breathe in the wonders that surrounds us as we passed by and our presence unaffected them.

"You seem to be deep in thought."

Ellie's voice woke me from my reverie that I forgot that I was not alone then I lovingly gazed at her and smiled, "I have a lot on my mind lately."

"Would you like to share it with me?" she asked sincerely with a hint of concern.

I didn't want her to worry so I lied, "it's nothing really, nothing to fuss about," I assured her dismissively.

Ellie suddenly stopped then stared right into my eyes like she was searching for something.

"You're lying," she softly accused.

"What made you say that?" I defended.

"Because I could tell and you're bad at it."

I softly chuckled and held her hand, "I couldn't tell you all the same."

I saw the disappointment in her face but she nodded telling me that she understood.

"Soon things will change Ellie, I don't know how or when but honestly, it is not too late for us to back out now if you decide to change your mind." I added sincerely hoping that she knew I didn't want her in any danger.

She squeezed my hand gently and responded, "We made it this far and we can't back out now. People's lives are depending on you," she explained then added, "I'm not leaving you, and if we get caught, I am prepared to face the consequences."

I gave her a huge smile and she smiled in return. I was proud of her and at the same time feared for her safety, and I hoped the day we face the consequences would never come. I slowly leaned towards her and placed a gentle kiss on her soft lips letting the rush overcome me.

"I love you Ellie," I confessed in a whisper as I lightly leaned my forehead on hers. The words came out of nowhere and it felt so right and easy, "I couldn't imagine a life without you. I couldn't understand how I could have lived my life before I met you," I continued.

Ellie didn't say anything when we gazed at each other, she just smiled affectionately but her silence didn't bother me, and as long as she knew my true feelings for her that was enough.

We were suddenly interrupted by Miss Pattilyn whose face were flushed from running, "My Lord! My Lady! Such terrible news! Terrible indeed!" she declared urgently while catching her breath, "There was an explosion at the Steel Plants and it was reported that the Defiers did it."

Ellie shifted her gaze at me without saying a word, and I silently looked at her intently.

The Protectors doubled their efforts patrolling the villages and towns in search for the Defiers responsible for the explosion of the Steel Plants. The incident halted the operations which only made Andrew's fury worst. The plan pushed through, our efforts were finally realized and thankfully no one was injured since it happened before dawn when it was still dark. There was chaos when the Protectors round up the people demanding them, often forcibly, to go out from their houses while the Protectors search their homes for any signs that they helped a Defier or for any evidence that they were a Defier themselves. Villagers were pushed around and those who refused to cooperate or for no reason at all were force to kneel or were beaten up, and I was there on behalf of the Duke with Captain Furlong to give the orders and made sure the perpetuators were found. We interrogated everybody and those who were found suspicious were taken away on to a shuttle to be interrogated further in prison. They looked at me with hatred and anger while I oversaw the Protectors and their brutality with no remorse or guilt or even pity on my face as I pretend to do my part as Lord of Pinewood. The news of the explosion had spread across the Empire and everybody was restless regardless of station. The Omegas and Betas were terrified while the Elites and Alphas grew sterner.

We were at the First Village and disorder followed us. The villagers were more uncooperative and more resistant making the Protectors use extreme force on them. Faces were beaten with the blunt handle of the Protector's firearm; some knelt on their knees defeated while others tried to fight back as they raged on. This time Captain Furlong ordered the Protectors to round up everybody to the village square. Women and children cried, terrified of their fate, as they were taken against their will while some were dragged away. Captain Furlong and I stood at the center of the square while the frightened villagers encircled us guarded by the Protectors. The angry ones grew restless and agitated, and spoke their objections on the situation, then an officer who was not far from where we stood, took out his handgun and aimed it above then fired one shot in the air. The loud noise finally silenced the crowd.

"You all know why you are here," Captain Furlong shouted with his loud strong voice, "Harboring traitors is treason and is against the law punishable by death," he continued while staring at the crowd with his cold face, "But if you give them up, his Grace the Duke will show leniency to you and your family," he added.

The crowd stood still in silence while the Captain continued to stare with his silent threats and I saw he grew impatient. He took a deep breath and let out a sigh then shouted, "Your silence will be the end of you."

There was a sudden stir among the crowd then voices of cries and protest were heard when Protectors shoved to make way for villagers that they dragged towards the center, then they were lined up in front of the crowd and the sixth and last villager to be brought forward was a familiar face, and it was Mr. James Conolly. His face remained strong but his eyes showed fear. He was then brought to the middle away from the others. I suddenly felt very uneasy especially since I was not made aware what was going to happen. Mr. Conolly briefly glanced at me but I stood there silently.

"You see these people here?" the Captain spoke, "If you give us the Defiers, then no harm will come to them," he declared in a menacing voice. The crowd protested while some pleaded for the lives of the villagers who were in front.

"Please Captain," Mr. Conolly pleaded, "These people are innocent."

Captain Furlong ignored his plea while he continued to stand with a forbidding appearance as the skies grew dark. Then I saw Mrs. Conolly and Hannah amongst the crowd crying and pleading for him.

I was troubled and the feeling grew increasingly that I couldn't stand here and just watch so I calmly suggested to the Captain, "Perhaps Captain if we could take them now to the shuttles, prison will surely change their minds," I said trying to make sure that my voice didn't hint of any signs of concern hoping that he would concede and this ordeal will be over with.

The Captain briefly looked at me and responded in a low voice, "Perhaps my Lord," but he continued to stand there without any intention of moving.

"Once again! Tell us where the Defiers are and His Grace will be lenient to you," the Captain repeated in a more grave voice.

The crowd shouted louder and Mr. Conolly pleaded again, "Mercy for us Captain! My Lord!" as he became more terrified. The Captain stood still and silent and his indifference remained that it was difficult to read what he was thinking. He was a hard military man and that was probably why he was Captain and rose to the ranks of the Alphas. He finally stirred then walked towards Mr. Conolly and he stood there studying him closely then he coldly said, "Mercy it is," in a blink of an eye he took out his hand gun from his side buckle then aimed it at Mr. Conolly's temple then pulled the trigger. The crowd was mortified with horror then chilling screams filled the air as Mr. Conolly's blood splattered and he fell on the ground lifeless. There was havoc as I stood there frozen staring down at his motionless body.

CHAPTER 13: HOMEWARD

ELAINE

The house became dismal of late. The hallways were empty and had a dispirited aura. The weather grew gloomy as a shadow spread over the land and more Protectors who were heavily armed patrolled these areas. Curtis grew more distant by the day and I tried to comfort him as he blames himself for everything. The loss of Mr. Conolly deeply affected him and it was hard to soothe away his pain when I myself felt disheartened as him. It was the first time I saw him like this and the way he was hurting was slowly destroying me. When I heard what happened to Mr. Conolly, my heart broke for his mate and daughter, the loss of a loved one was the hardest thing to bear.

I was on my way to Curtis' private office hoping that I would catch him there and see if he was feeling better. I knew he preferred to be alone, and I gave him the space if it meant it would help him overcome the loss but I would check on him from time to time in case he needed someone to talk to. I arrived at his office and the door was wide opened. He looked up from his desk when I shut the door and approached him. I could see dark circles around his eyes and he looked tired but he did his best to smile when he saw me.

"Ellie! Glad you're here, I was about to go looking for you," he said enthusiastically.

I took a seat in front of him and smiled then asked sweetly, "Do you need anything?"

He shook his head then responded, "Before I tell you, I want to apologize first for not being myself lately, I was in a difficult place...." his voice trailed off.

"It's okay Curtis, you don't need to explain anything to me. I just want to be there for you," I tenderly reassured him.

He smiled then stood and walked over to the chair beside me and sat there then he gently held my hands, "Thank you Ellie," then he softly planted a kiss on my hand.

Then his mood changed to a more cheerful note, "I have good news for you," he declared.

"Oh? That would be the first," I jested smiling.

He laughed and continued, "I finally secured us a passage to Coastal City."

At first I was not sure what he was saying or what he meant. He must have noticed my confusion when he added excitedly, "We're going to visit your home Ellie!"

I was dumbstruck and didn't respond immediately, "But how did you manage it?" I stuttered.

He laughed at my stunned face then he explained, "Well I made an excuse to Andrew that we needed help if we're going to catch the Defiers and we had connections at Coastal City so I told him I should go and bring you along with me. I told him that all that was happening with the Defiers and all were taking its toll on you and you needed to unwind. Of course he did not agree at first but then I told him that maybe you will give a good word to the Prince about him in return for this favor, and it seemed to work," he grinned.

I was ecstatic of the thought of going back home again that it felt unreal. Never in my wildest dreams would I have thought to return there after what happened to me and Andrew. I finally could go back where I truly belonged and see mom and dad again. I was so grateful for

Curtis for this wonderful gift, that he made me so happy. I became excited then asked him, "So when are we leaving?"

The sun was high on the clear sky, and the ocean was calm as the heat of the day engulfed the breeze. I heard the waves lazily hit the shores of the beach and the sound of seagulls as they were flying freely. I smelled the salt in the tame wind while I stood on the balcony. This was home, although I have never been on this part of the city but it was all too familiar as well. We stayed at the other side of the city where the Elites' ravishing apartments on the beach were and each more magnificent. It was owned by Curtis' family and one of the largest and the most elegant in the area. The turquoise blue stone walls and white marbles played well together in the hallway. Unlike the manor where art paintings and portraits were everywhere but in here there was no need for one because the large windows and balcony had the breathtaking view of the wide vast ocean, and everything was subtle and peaceful. Curtis joined on the balcony and stood beside me enjoying the breeze.

"The most beautiful view in the house," Curtis softly declared.

"It is," I agreed grinning but when I turned to him, he was lovingly gazing at me and not the view. He was beaming and I awkwardly laughed then we continued standing there in silence. His mood changed for the better ever since we arrived, and I could see he was happy and was slowly returning to his old self again that it gave me joy sharing this experience with him.

"I could imagine a day here would be that I would stare at the ocean and think of its wonderful mysteries beneath, or how the weather brightens the mood. The people around have their own stories to tell but it will remain an intriguing mystery and the structures has its own history and are all connected despite its size or origin. And all these splendid beauty around us deserved to be marveled as it should be.... And you Ellie are a part of it," he sincerely declared.

I gazed at him smiling and I suddenly felt embarrassed but his words felt so good, "That's a bit dramatic isn't it?" I teased trying to change the mood.

He laughed hard then finally admitted, "Well it's the truth," he shrugged.

It felt good feeling this way, away from Pinewood, away from the pain and suffering we had to endure back there. I felt so free and I think he felt the same way too. He was leaning on the concrete railing of the balcony and stared at the ocean when I gazed at him. Sometimes I could see the pain in his eyes whenever he was deep in thought and I wanted to help him with that.

"We've been talking mostly about me. I think it's time that we talked about you," I said tenderly and I gently placed my hand over his that he laid on the railing.

He softly smiled, "What do you want to know?"

"Everything."

I could barely contain my excitement when we were on our way to my house; it even kept me awake all night. Curtis who was with me couldn't help but looked thrilled too. I felt sorry for him though that he lost both his parents but I was glad when we finally had the chance to talk about them. He shared about his disappointments with his father, his love for his mother and his resentments towards Andrew. I think he needed someone to talk to, and his face showed that he was contented to have finally spoken about it. When we got closer, everything in the neighborhood remained the same and familiar. We eventually parked outside my house and the people nearby started noticing the expensive car then I glanced without meaning to at the bakery from across the street and I didn't know why I did that. Did I hope to see him there? But I'm with Curtis now I told myself.

"Are you ready?" Curtis asked interrupting my thoughts.

I nodded excitedly then we proceeded to get out from the car. A little crowd started to form around us, Curtis went out first and then I followed, and when I stood at the sidewalk I heard gasp from the neighbors who were looking and I could hear them say my name in hushed voice to the person beside them. Some stared at Curtis and others at me which felt very uncomfortable. We went towards the door and before we could knock I saw mom open it ecstatic with tears to see me. She immediately gave me a hug and dad was behind her beaming almost in tears. We entered the house and my tears started to form in my eyes as well.

"Oh my Ellie! Look how beautiful you are, being a Lady suits you, and your dress…." Mom happily declared while staring at what I wore. It was a short pastel blue dress that flowed freely and white heels, and she was not used to me wearing clothes like this but this was not a Lady's dress though, this dress actually broke protocol but I never did cared and I didn't see the point on sticking out in this neighborhood wearing such extravagant clothing. Curtis was kind enough too to dress comfortably and not on Lord's clothes.

"Can I give my little girl a hug?" dad cheerfully asked then we hug so tight that my tears started to flow.

"I'm so happy to see you dad," I happily declared crying.

"There Ellie, your home now," he said in a soothing voice then he asked, "Well aren't you going to introduce us to your Lord?"

Dad was smiling and mom was beaming when I introduced them to Curtis who was pleasantly gracious enough to shake their hands. We were at the kitchen eating our lunch and nothing had change in the house, it was still cozy just like the day I left it. We were enjoying each other's company and talked mostly what mom and dad had been doing since I left. I found out that I became popular around here and some were proud that a Beta turned Elite was their neighbor, and mom claimed that people were much friendly to her since then. Both of them expressed their happiness that I'm doing well at Pinewood and gave their gratitude to Curtis for taking good care of me. I also told them how we met the Crowned Prince and they were amazed and in awe especially mom who kept asking a lot of questions. Then we laughed some more and I glanced at Curtis who was clearly enjoying this too, and I have never saw him this happy before. We spent the afternoon together in the house. Dad and Curtis talked about politics while mom was at the kitchen. I looked out the window in front of the house and I saw people were going through their usual business. Then for a while I saw him across the street but then I realized it was a different man sweeping outside the bakery. It was then that I knew that he was gone, probably matched with another Omega. I felt relief that he was not there actually but some parts of me misses him. He belonged to my past and that life was long gone.

  I continued to spend my days here in Coastal City,

I cherished every moment of it knowing that I might leave again someday. Curtis didn't mentioned though how long we were staying and I didn't dare asked. He was very generous when he offered that I stayed with my parents and he at the apartment but he drops by everyday to spend some time with me. I didn't know where he goes and when I asked he would just answer that he had some business he had to attend to, and besides there were times when I was glad that he wasn't around the house because mom blurts out embarrassing topics like when she asked about grandchildren and I would answer her that we haven't talked about it and I wanted her to drop the subject but she was persistent.

"What's there to talk about? They just draw both of your blood at the clinic then you wait for five months for the fetus to fully develop," she explained.

"Well we're just not yet ready for that kind of responsibility," I defended.

Those were my usual days with mom when she was not at work but when I spend my time with dad, it was a whole different conversation. I brought him back to the apartment so that we can spend our day together at the beach. It was his first time there since nobody was ever allowed except for the Elites because beaches were very valuable property that only the Elites could afford to stay. Dad was in awe when he arrived; he always thought he would never step foot in a place like this. It felt strange how quickly our lives changed when I became an Elite. We walked along the shores just the two of us holding our shoes feeling the waves between our toes.

"So how's your life Ellie?" he asked.

"I'm good dad," I answered.

"I am so glad to hear that. Your mom and I were very

worried when we left you at the ceremony."

"It was hard but I managed."

He chuckled, "You always do."

We continued to walk in silence.

"I didn't want to talk about this in front of your mother but I heard the news about the explosion in Pinewood," he stated worriedly.

"We're fine dad," I reassured giving a soft laugh to convince him that it was nothing to worry about but he suddenly stopped walking and I did the same then he turned to face me.

"Ellie, you're an Elite now. People there might see you differently and would try to hurt you. They will see you as one of them. I just want you safe. You're always welcome at home if ever trouble comes for you," he said sincerely with a worried look.

I gave him my warmest smile then hugged him and said, "Thank you dad."

I was in our living room reminiscing with mom and dad that night when there was a soft knock on our door. Dad opened it and Curtis appeared then he was asked to come in which he willingly did.

"Can I get you anything my Lord? Coffee or tea?" mom pleasantly offered.

"As much as I would like to take you up on that offer Mrs. Gertrude but sadly I couldn't stay long," Curtis regretfully apologized, "I came here to ask if I could have a word with Ellie privately if it's alright?" he added.

"Of course my Lord. Ellie don't keep him waiting," mom urged.

"We can talk in my room," I offered.

It felt awkward bringing Curtis up here. It was far beyond the size of our chambers back in Pinewood. It had a single bed, a little one door closet and a small table where a mirror was and a chair. It barely fit the two of us inside but I saw Curtis was not bothered of the size as he took a seat on the chair while I sat on the bed.

"I am sorry I interrupted your night with your parents but I had to tell you something that couldn't wait," he stated with some urgency.

"It's fine, they won't mind," I assured him.

There was hesitation and a look of concern on his face before he proceeded.

"I'm leaving for Gelhem tomorrow," he finally said.

I was confused, "What's in Gelhem?"

"Just more business that's why I need you to stay with your parents for a while."

I would love nothing more but to stay here, but I couldn't help feeling that he was hiding something.

"You're going to Gelhem.... and leaving me here... but you told Andrew that you're staying here with me.... something does not add up," I said trying to put the pieces together.

Curtis sighed then shook his head, "I can't seem to hide anything from you can I?" he stated, "I can't tell you so that's that," he added firmly.

"Why do you always do this? Always hiding everything from me?" I asked as I was starting to get annoyed.

"Because you're too stubborn sometimes!" he declared a bit louder than what I was used to then he looked frustrated. Was this our first fight together? I didn't say another word, and then he rubbed his face against his palm as he bent over his chair but then sat up straight as he composed himself and then I noticed his distress.

"I'm sorry Ellie I shouldn't have shouted like that," he sincerely apologized, "I just think it will be better if you didn't know," he continued.

I paused trying to figure this out then I asked in a whisper, "This is about the Defiers isn't?"

He stared at me refusing to answer.

"I thought we were in this together?"

"It's too dangerous," he finally answered in a calm voice.

"Then I'm coming with you and you can't stop me," I insisted firmly while I saw the frown on Curtis' defeated face.

CHAPTER 14: GELHEM

CURTIS

It was difficult to be conspicuous in the Fisherman's town of Gelhem. A busy town that strangers would blend in easily and the clothes we wore were almost identical to theirs. Loose plain pants and shirts in dull colors with no special design whatsoever that we wore underneath our long brown cloak. I was not happy that Ellie had to come along, she was safer back at Coastal City but then she kept insisting and our argument grew more intense that I had to concede defeat. I was furious at her but I knew I couldn't stay mad. I saw her fearlessness as we walk through the town market, and she was always eager to visit a place where she had not been to. Gelhem's main source of income was fishes. People everywhere would come here to buy or sell all types of it of all sizes freshly caught from the ocean. The air would smell of salt and fish, and the ground was muddy and wet, but the skies showed that it was clear and sunny, and the structures were all made of out wood of dull dark colors, nothing was pleasant but Ellie didn't seem to care. The market was crowded and noisy as the people were trying to sell their fish while a buyer bargains the price. There were some who would clean the fish for you and threw its guts on the ground where stray dogs and cats would gather along with the flies.

We reached what looked like the town's inn and there was a sign that said they were serving food so we decided to go in to eat and stay away from the market. The place was crowded but we found an empty table near the window then we took off our cloaks and sat down. I scanned the room and there was nobody there that I recognized. Most of the people were talking loudly among themselves and not caring for those around them. Then a plump woman finally approached us wearing her plain dress, an apron which was clearly had not been washed, and her expression showed that she was more annoyed that we even bother coming inside.

"What are you having?" she snapped while she placed a strand of curly brown unkempt hair behind her ear as it tried to escape her head piece made out of white cloth to hold her hair.

"What are you serving?" I asked grinning trying to be charming.

"Fish!," she blurted angrily.

I hesitated then asked in a most respectful way, "Do you have anything besides fish?" then I smiled widely.

It only made her temper worst but before she could say something Ellie quickly interrupted her, "We'll take the fish," then she smiled.

The woman glared at Ellie then finally said, "I'll be back with it," she muttered.

Ellie waited for the woman to leave then she asked me, "Who are we looking for?"

"You'll see," I replied.

After a while, we finished our meal then left some money on the table and as we stood up and were about to leave the grumpy woman came back and whispered subtly something to us while she took our plates.

"Go to the docks, there's a small fishing storage there at the end. He will be waiting." After that she took the money on the table then left.

We headed to the docks and it was a relief that it was less crowded. Some fishermen stored their cleaned gears as they prepared to leave while some folded their fishing nets. We reached the storage at the end of the dock and nobody was around. I held the door handle but before I opened I glanced at Ellie and she gave me a silent nod telling me that she was ready for whatever was behind it. I pushed the door open and it made a creaking sound. It was full of fishing nets and gears then we slowly went inside the dark room only lit by the sun passing between the wooden planks on the wall. Nobody was inside.

Then there was a sound of heavy footsteps on the dock approaching us. Ellie immediately went behind me as we waited to see who was coming. Then a huge figure stood outside the doorway

"Glad you're here," Olfren's deep voice greeted us, "Is she coming?" he asked referring to Ellie.

"Yes, is that going to be a problem?" I responded.

Olfren shrugged, "No problem with me. Come on then."

He led us to a small fishing boat and there was a man already on board making preparations. Olfren stood beside the boat then said, "Hop on." I got on first then assisted Ellie and then Olfren followed. The man loosened up the rope that was holding the boat to the docks then went over to the helm and turned on the engine. It made a choking sound at first then slowly roared to life. The boat was rusty and old but it didn't have any problem floating as it slowly left the dock.

"By the way, I need you two to go below deck. It's cramp but you'd be comfortable enough. We don't want to catch anybody's attention," Olfren stated and we obliged silently.

Below deck was a small space that could barely fit four

people. There were fishing gears and a dirty white hammock hanging above the nets, and farther inside it was full of clutter and a small wooden table and a bench on each side. We took a seat across from each other as the boat slowly rocked while we sailed on what seemed to be almost half an hour.

I looked at Ellie and asked, "Are you okay?" sounding concerned.

"I'm fine," she replied softly.

I gently took her hands and held them. "I don't know if we'll be safe where we are going but if you see something suspicious or anything wrong, I want you to run, just run don't worry about me," I spoke stressing the importance of my words.

She smiled warmly and responded, "Nothing is going to happen."

Footsteps came down the stairs and as we looked to see who it was, Olfren appeared.

"How's our Lord and Lady?" he asked cheerfully.

"How far are we?" I anxiously asked.

"Oh we're almost there," he answered placing his right foot on top of a wooden box that was on the floor and held a rope that was dangling from the ceiling to support himself while the boat swayed. He leaned towards us and continued, "Once we arrived just do what I say. The journey isn't that long but it's not going to be comfortable."

"Alright," I agreed and Ellie silently nodded.

"Good!" he said contented.

There was a sudden loud foot stomp that came from above and what sounded like the man on the wheel shouted, "We're here."

Olfren then straightened himself up and he was about to go above deck when he turned back to us and said solemnly, "I'm sorry about James Conolly, he was a good man."

"He was," I agreed nodding.

The boat was nearing what looked like a small abandoned wooden dock almost hidden amongst heavy bushes growing freely on the rocks. The boat's engine died down as we slowly drifted towards it. Olfren jumped off first holding a rope then quickly tied it to the dock and the boat slowly rocked when we completely stopped. I quickly took a look around but I saw no one but the sight of thick bushes made me anxious knowing that somebody might be behind those. I held my hand out for Ellie to help her off the boat. We were on the ground when Olfren told us, "We're not going to be taking any breaks so keep up." He led the way and we followed slowly with me on the rear making our way through the large rocks and bushes. The sun was upon us as we moved forward through the thick bushes and trees while I moved branches that were on my way. Sounds from unfamiliar birds and insects were the only noise I could hear and my breath as the heat began to worsen but Ellie's pace did not falter as she effortlessly kept up with Olfren. It felt like time stood still here as everything looked the same, the trees and bushes and even the path. After a while of walking, Ellie was beside me and without taking her eyes off Olfren she asked in a whisper, "How do you know him?"

I glanced at Olfren then responded in a hushed tone, "He found me back in Pinewood then he gave me a choice." I recalled to her the day I first met Olfren and ever since then my life was never the same.

"It was a good choice though," she grinned.

"I hope so," I grinned back

"We're getting close," Olfren suddenly declared.
In front of us was a mountain covered mostly in rocks and it was not that high. I scanned the area and no one was around, and I didn't see any camp or any signs that the Defiers were even here.

"Should we climb up?" Ellie asked.

"That's far enough," a stranger's voice suddenly spoke. Four armed men came out of nowhere and pointed their firearms at us.

"Hey no need for that, they're with me," Olfren explained while he positioned himself between us and the armed men. The man in front studied us then he finally commanded, "Weapons down," and the others obeyed. "Search them," he then added.

Two men came forward, one searched me for any concealed weapons then one approached Ellie but she gave him a stern look and then Olfren intervene saying, "She's clean."

"You know the protocol Olfren," the man said.

"But I still outrank you here Thomas," Olfren stated grinning.

Thomas gave him a grave look then seemed to calm down and finally said, "Follow me."

We went around the mountain then when we reached the other side the men suddenly stopped. Thomas motioned his head at one of his men who hurriedly obeyed and knelt one knee on the ground and was searching under the leaves and grass for something. He stopped when I saw his hand was on a small metal plate that was covered with dirt then he flipped it open and a black button was inside. He pressed it and the ground slowly shook. In front of us the ground split opened revealing a path going down below which looked like a dark cave. The man who opened it went down first then I heard a click and there were lights inside revealing another path. The men started descending one at a time. Olfren went first then Ellie, and I glanced at Thomas and he gestured his head for me to go down. When I was inside, I heard another click from behind me then I saw the ground shook again and the wide exit was shut tight. We moved forward and as we went farther, the more we descended. The path eventually led us to a huge cave; some parts of the walls and ceilings were covered in iron sheets. The place was well lighted with white lights hanging on the ceiling and tube lights ran along the walls. The unusual part in the cave was that there were people. They were working and some were carrying small boxes while instructed by someone holding a clipboard, and others were fixing something that looked like an engine.

"Wait here," Olfren suddenly instructed and so we stood our ground. He left us with Thomas as we disappeared farther beyond the boxes. He returned shortly after and with him was a tall woman with long blonde curly hair, and she was smiling cheerfully when she approached.

"Finally you're here!" she excitedly stated.

"Lord Curtis, Lady Elaine, this is Allison," Olfren introduced.

Allison smiled brightly, "Nice meeting you!"

"Nice to meet you too Allison," Ellie greeted and smiled in return.

I just glanced at her while feeling suspicious of everything.

"I know you two have a lot of questions but you must be tired. How about a rest first," Allison happily offered.

I might feel tired but I didn't come here to take a rest.

I felt impatient especially in a place where I did not trust the people, and time was not our ally at this moment.

"I would rather meet the person in charge of all this," I admitted trying not to sound that it was a suggestion.

Allison's mood slightly changed but maintained her smile and said, "Oh okay, I'll take you to see Ryder then."

We followed Allison and Olfren farther into the cave and came upon a hallway where we passed more people. We stopped in front of a metal door then Allison knocked and I heard from inside a voice who asked, "What?" Allison then opened the door and we entered following her, there was a long metal table at the middle and sitting across from each other was a man and a woman, and it seemed that we interrupted them. The man with short balding blonde hair and a stern look spoke first scowling, "I told you not now."

"They asked to see Ryder now," Allison explained who suddenly lost her cheerfulness.

They were silent then the man finally said, "Fine let them in."

Allison ushered us inside and then she left. We took a seat at the long table with Olfren joining us on the other side. The woman who had a very short silver hair, and a hint of wrinkles under her eyes continued to stare at us. She had an intimidating aura around her by the hardened expression, and straight posture she possessed.

"Lord Curtis, I would like to say thank you for coming and we appreciate your assistance at Pinewood, it helped us a great deal," the man spoke after we took our seats.

I didn't say anything and continued to look at him and the woman from across.

He cleared his throat then continued to speak, "We asked you to come here because we need your help and it's not just in Pinewood."

"I don't know how I can help you outside of Pinewood," I hesitantly admitted.

The man studied me from where he sat then spoke, "The Defiers have been around since even you were born. We are all over silently working in the shadows, waiting for the right opportunity, and since its existence never have we had an Elite among our ranks. Someone of your station could give us information and access to what we lacked, and your connections and power could greatly help our cause and could save people's lives."

I was confused then I asked, "I don't understand, what are you planning after Pinewood?"

"The Empire," the woman suddenly spoke her voice stern.

I looked at her, and when I knew what they wanted from me I became tense. They want me to help them destroy the Empire but that was too much. The Empire was too powerful with the vast of Corps serving under the Emperor; an attack would be futile. Ellie, who sat beside me, gently placed her hand on mine and I glanced at her and I saw her eyes gazing directly at me.

"What if I refuse," I asked turning back to them.

The woman shifted her stare from me to Ellie then answered, "Then we're hoping she would."

"No," I objected shaking my head with my agitation starting to rise.

"It's not for you to decide," the woman declared.

Then I turned to Ellie and softly squeezed her hand and looking into her eyes hoping she would not accept. Ellie looked at me then finally answered, "I'll only do it if Curtis is with me."

I turned to the man and said, "There, you got your answer. Now can we leave?" I demanded anxiously.

"Not yet," the woman spoke. Then I became confuse then frustrated staring at the woman then at the man and asked, "Who's in charge in here anyway?"

"I am," the woman answered calmly and sterner, "I am Ryder and this is my second in command Quinlan."

Ryder sighed then she continued, "Pinewood is not the only one suffering. There are more places being oppressed under the rule of the Empire and will continue to do so unless we do something and the only way to create absolute change is to target our focus on the Empire itself that had placed unjust laws for generations." She paused and glanced at me then Ellie then resumed solemnly, "I believe that when the time would come to fight back, it would be for equality, not for power or wealth. To be born entitled to the freedom to choose, to have the right to follow your dreams, and not to be destined to a path already written for you by unworthy hands. Soon our lives would not be defined by our stations but by our choices."

I sat there in silence contemplating then I gazed at Ellie. I could see in her eyes that she believed her words. Although Ryder spoke the truth, I just couldn't help feel that this was impossible, I didn't see the point in all of this, there would be a lot of casualties if we go against the Empire itself and if we did this, how could we win with just a few Defiers?

"Perhaps...." Olfren suddenly spoke, "some further persuasion might help."

We returned to the hallway following Ryder and Olfren and I took my time looking around while we walked. "That's the training room," Olfren exclaimed nodding at the direction to an open room full of training equipment and weapons for physical assault.

"And across from it is the shooting gallery," he added.

"This here is the mess hall," he pointed at large place with no doors full of long wooden tables and benches with lights hanging from the high cave ceiling which was supported by huge metal beams. The floors and walls were covered with plain metal sheets and with no windows. The food counter was on the other side of a corner where I could see people busily preparing the next meal. The hallway started to descend some more as we continued. "And finally this is our living quarters," he proudly declared. My eyes widened at the vastness of the cave that was before me. The cave on these parts went circular and we entered at the middle of it. You could see large spiral metal beams going around the cave from the top then down to the lowest level, it was built on the walls which became the floors as well on each level, which I counted there were ten, and it had metal railings in placed along the edge, and on each level were wooden doors but no windows; there were stairs that was carved on the cave walls that takes you up or down to the quarters. Small lights were on the walls but what astonished me was that the sun shone in here. When I looked up, I saw a thick clear glass, and big enough to let the sun shine through to the center on the lowest level of the living quarters where people were gathered talking and sitting around the tables and chairs enjoying each other's company. We were descending to the lower levels while I kept on studying the glass above.

"It's a reflection," Olfren suddenly spoke.

I gave him a puzzled look.

"Some clever folks around here decided to brightened up the place so they built a mirror on top of the mountain that would follow the sun and capture its rays then reflect it to a bunch of other mirrors placed on a precise calculated position underneath the mountain and the rays would bounce on them until it reaches here," he pointed up at the large glass," he explained grinning.

"It's impressive," I commented.

When we reached the bottom where the people were gathered, Allison saw us then left the group she was conversing with and came bounding towards us.

"Is it time?" she asked excitedly to Ryder.

Ryder didn't answer but nodded her head. We followed Allison and headed to the only large metal door in the quarters. It automatically split open when we approached, and inside was a brightly lit room which looked like an infirmary. The floors and walls were covered in metal sheets, and the beds were clean and medical equipment and medicines were all organized. At the corner, where a desk and stools could be found, was a young woman, a man, and a child sitting and talking but stopped when they saw us approaching.

"You guys have been waiting long?" Allison asked happily.

The child, a little girl with brown hair and brown eyes spoke first, "Not that long Alli," she sweetly replied. The other one a young woman with long black hair who looked bored and uninterested was crossing her arms while sitting and rolled her eyes. The man with unkempt light brown hair who looked older than the others smiled and said, "We were just catching up on things."

Allison beamed then spoke, "Let me introduce you guys to our guest, this is Lord Curtis and Lady Elaine."

"Hi," Ellie greeted smiling widely.

I gave a soft smile without saying a word since I was

unsure on why we were here and who they were.

The little girl seemed to be interested in Ellie that her face lit up and said, "Hi I'm Jilly."

Ellie went closer to her and said happily, "Nice to meet you Jilly, you can call me Ellie."

Jilly was beaming and then she giggled then Allison continued with the introduction, "This is Celine,"

"Hey," greeted the young woman with less enthusiasm.

"And that's Richard," added Allison, referring to the man who smiled with confidence and nodded.

"Where's Doctor Irene?" Ryder inquired, but before anybody could answer, the metal door opened then a woman in a white coat appeared and was talking to someone who was following behind her.

"Just try to sleep on your left side Sarah," a woman with braided long black hair and bronze skin didn't notice us when she entered.

"I'll try to remember that doctor," a voice of a woman from behind the doctor responded.

When the second woman entered, I was in shock and bewildered, and I couldn't stop staring at the woman's midsection which was enlarged. At first I thought she might be ill but she looked happy and healthy. My trance broke when I realized someone was talking to me.

"You must be the people Olfren was talking about. I'm Doctor Irene," said the woman in the white coat, "And this is Sarah," she added referring to the woman who I was staring.

"Hello," Sarah greeted shyly.

Ellie was the only one who had the strength to ask the question that I couldn't, "Is she…. Pregnant?"

"Yes seven months to be exact," replied Doctor Irene

with such professionalism.

"But.... How?...." Ellie stuttered in amazement.

"Honestly, we don't know. We have many theories, one of them was that Sarah may not have been given the sterility serum while she was in the Birth Chamber," Doctor Irene explained.

"That's impossible! The serum is needed for her to survive in the chamber," Ellie commented.

"Yes that's what we thought so too or maybe Sarah's body reacted differently to the serum." The doctor explained further.

Ryder suddenly spoke, "The sterility serum is one of the ways the Empire is controlling us, the stations, the Numen system, everything, but here we have the future, the Premortals."

"The Premortals?" I asked curiously.

Ryder nodded, "Yes we call them that because we do not know how these infants came to be when their mothers were born in the Birth Chambers. For more than decades, we found who was probably the first and believed there could be more who were born by their mothers but they have been in hiding ever since. Richard, Celine, and Jilly are our Premortals and we have one more on the way," she nodded at the direction of Sarah, "And this became the driving force for the Defiers," she added.

Jilly ran towards Sarah and gently hugged her belly and said sweetly, "I love you mom," and Sarah smiled in return.

Everything I just heard seemed impossible but I was here and the proof was standing before me. Although I was finding it hard to grasp the reality of this all but I knew what I had to do.

Ellie approached Sarah and Jilly then pleasantly said, "I'm so happy for you both!"

Sarah beamed and shyly responded, "Thank you."

"Is there any way we could know the gender?" Ellie asked curiously.

"There's no way of knowing since we lost the technology long before any of this," Doctor Irene answered.

I saw in Ellie's expression that she was deep in thought then after a moment she glanced at me and she had a look of determination in her then she glanced at Ryder saying, "I know what I have to do now but I need Curtis to be with me on this."

Ellie returned her gaze back at me and her eyes told me that she had made a decision and I cannot persuade her otherwise then without saying any word I nodded then turned to Ryder and I told her something that I was not sure until this moment, "I'm in, I want to help."

They broke into their happy faces except for Ryder who remained staring at me intently.

"We need to get back before it gets late," I declared anxiously and regretfully that I had to end this.

"Please stay for a while," Allison begged.

"I wish we could but it's too dangerous if we stay any longer," I stated.

"You could at least take a break while we prepare the route for your safe return. There's still time right Ryder?" Allison turned to Ryder pleading.

Ryder nodded and said, "Yes there's time."

"Actually, I don't mind staying for a bit," Ellie admitted.

Allison was ecstatic when she got what she wanted.

We were at the mess hall with Allison, Jilly, Celine and Richard waiting for our escort to take us back.

Ellie was willing and happy talking with them that she had so many questions. We found out that the Premortals had been in hiding all their lives with their mothers and fathers, and have never been to the institutions or matched since they were not citizens of the Empire. They also shared what it was like to live here under the cave. Despite their limited spaces, they all seemed happy. They eventually left when Olfren arrived and told them that it was almost time for us to go, then Allison asked us to wait here for a while she makes the final preparations with Olfren. Then it was just the two of us in the mess hall seated beside each other.

"Can you believe all this?" I asked in awe.

"I know, it's hard to sink in," Ellie agreed smiling.

"You know," I said in a solemn voice, "everything is going to change after this. The dangers are going to be far more greater," I declared worriedly.

"Don't worry, you're not alone. I will save you if ever you need saving," she assured me beaming.

I chuckled, "Since when do you save an Elite?"

She giggled, "You're not an Elite anymore, the moment you went down this cave, you renounced your station and everything."

I was silent for a while before I replied, "You're right.... Would you still be with me if I lose everything?"

She laughed, "Then you'll live in a cave like this one?" she teased.

"Yes," I replied in a serious tone looking down at the table.

Ellie noticed my tone then she moved closer, her shoulder touched mine then she gently placed her hand on my face and turned me to face her then she lovingly said, "Then I'll go with you." Her face slowly leaned towards mine and our lips found each other as we locked into a kiss that she passionately gave that I have never felt from her before, it engulfed me like a flame. I didn't want it stop but a stranger's voice had to ruin it.

"Ellie??"

She immediately broke the kiss and briefly turned to hide her embarrassed expression and then she faced to see who had just called her and that was when I saw her reaction turned to utter shock.

------ TO BE CONTINUED ------

Sequel Coming Soon

ABOUT THE AUTHOR

Jacqueline Wrenley

manages her family's hotel and restaurant in Bohol, Philippines. Writing stories is her hobby. The Premortals was revised and completed on April 2020 while she was on home quarantine due to the COVID-19 virus outbreak. This is her first novel.

Made in the USA
San Bernardino, CA
23 April 2020